STEPH.

MW00927981

Courage and Faith

Stephen Curry: Courage and Faith

Copyright © 2017 All rights reserved to Sole Books Beverly Hills

No part of this book may be reproduced or transmitted in any form
or by any means, electronic or mechanical, including photocopying,
recording, or by any information storage or retrieval system, without
written permission from Sole Books. For information regarding
permission write to Sole Books, P.O. Box 10445, Beverly Hills,
CA 90213.

A special thank you to Yonatan, Yaron, and Guy Ginsberg.
Cover design: Omer Pikarski
Front cover picture: Gary A. Vasquez - USA TODAY Sports
Back cover picture: Jake Roth – USA TODAY Sports
Series editor: Y Ginsberg
Proof editor: Michele Caterina
Page layout design: Lynn M. Snyder

Library of Congress Cataloging-in-Publication data available.

ISBN: 978-1-938591-42-6
E-ISBN: 978-1-938591-52-5

Published by Sole Books, Beverly Hills, California
Printed in the United States of America
First edition July 2017

www.solebooks.com

STEPHEN CURRY
Courage and Faith

By

Rick Leddy

Eyes Wide Open

"ARE YOU SURE ABOUT THIS?" Dell Curry asked his wife, Sonya. "He's only two weeks old."

Dell knew what Sonya's answer would be even before she replied. Once Sonya made her mind up about something, it was pretty much a done deal. He was concerned that maybe she and little Stephen were going out into public a bit too soon. But what did he know? He was only 24 years old and this whole parent thing was entirely new and confusing to him.

Sonya was holding Stephen in her arms. She looked down at her son and smiled. Wardell Stephen Curry II. Named after his father. Steph had made quite a splash coming into the world. He had been born two weeks earlier than she or Dell had expected.

Dell, who was a sharpshooting guard for the Cleveland Cavaliers, had been in New York to play the New York Knicks when Sonya felt the pains and knew the baby was coming. When she called Dell from Akron, Ohio, to tell him the baby was on its way, he said he would try to get back as soon as possible. In the meantime, he advised her to call Brad Daughtery's girlfriend to drive her to the hospital. Brad was a teammate of Dell's.

Sonya had been scared. It was her first child and Dell wasn't with her. Neither she nor Brad's girlfriend were all that familiar with Akron. She and Dell had only been living in Akron for a few months.

When they finally arrived at the hospital, she discovered they had driven to the wrong one! After a police escort and a wild ride to the correct hospital, Sonya arrived only to find out there was no room available for her to have the baby in. A room was eventually found and, just two hours later, the boy she was now holding in her arms was born.

She looked at her two-week-old baby and then at Dell and said, "We are going to the game. Your son needs to see what his father does for a living. You are going to be away from home a lot and he needs to be a part of your life. And that starts now."

Sonya's words made Dell a bit sad. He still felt guilty for not being at the hospital when Stephen was born. He had gotten back as soon as he could, but it hadn't been soon enough.

Dell smiled and stared at his son sleeping quietly in Sonya's arms. How much would he really be able to enjoy a Cavaliers versus Chicago Bulls game? He was so tiny and looked so much like his mother, right down to the brown hazel eyes they both shared.

"Michael Jordan will be playing tonight, right?" Sonya said. "Do you think you could get him to autograph Stephen's blanket?"

Dell stood for a moment with his mouth open, unable to find words. Sonya burst out laughing and soon they were both laughing, then quickly stifled it when the baby stirred.

Dell had to get to Richfield Coliseum in Cleveland, where the Cavaliers played their home games, for pre-game warm-ups. Later, Sonya drove Stephen to the game herself and they got there just fine. Stephen slept the entire drive from Akron. He was still sleeping, wrapped up in his blanket as Sonya made her way to her seat. He slept through the well-wishers and the people who wanted to get a glance at the newly minted Wardell Stephen Curry II. He then slept through the team introductions and the loud music and the national anthem.

When the buzzer sounded to begin the game, Sonya looked down at the little bundle on her lap and noticed that his eyes were now wide open. *Well, well, little man, you woke up just in time to catch the game, huh?*

She figured that wouldn't last long, but was surprised when he stayed wide awake during the first quarter and then when his eyes were still wide open the whole second quarter. He even stayed awake for the entire halftime show. He didn't cry. She thought he looked genuinely *interested* in his surroundings. Sonya smiled. If she didn't know better, she could swear that he was actually enjoying himself, reveling in the NBA atmosphere. Maybe he was checking out how the best basketball players in the world astounded the crowd with their leaps, agility, and amazing shooting skills.

He'll wear out and fall asleep again soon, she thought.

But he didn't. He stayed awake for the third quarter and then the fourth. She made sure to whisper to Stephen whenever Dell was put into the game, "That's your Daddy out there. You watch him."

His eyes were *still* open during overtime, as the Bulls pulled out a last second 111–110 victory over the Cavs. Dell had every right to be proud of his premier outing in front of his son, scoring 24 points off the bench. Yet, Michael Jordan scored 39 points for the winning Bulls. After the game, Sonya made her way outside to the car and Stephen was still awake. She put him in the car seat and strapped him in and finally his eyes drooped sleepily and closed.

She was sitting in the passenger seat as she waited for Dell to leave the Cavs locker room and meet her at the car for the drive home back to Akron. She thought about her son sleeping peacefully in the car seat behind her. *What is*

God's plan for you, little boy, she thought as Dell approached the car.

As soon as Dell opened the car door, he leaned in and kissed Sonya. He quickly looked over the driver's seat to get a glimpse of his son. He smiled and gently touched Stephen's forehead, but couldn't completely hide a little disappointment.

"Aww, I thought he might be awake. I wanted him to see me play tonight," he whispered to Sonya.

Sonya replied, "Oh, he saw you tonight. Believe me. Have I got a story for you. I'll tell you on the ride back."

Dell looked at Sonya quizzically, worked himself into the driver seat and started the car to begin the journey home. But just as they were leaving the parking lot he noticed that Sonya had fallen asleep, too.

He sighed and figured the story could wait until they all got home.

Grandma Duckie's

WHEN STEPH WAS ONE YEAR OLD the Currys moved
to Charlotte, North Carolina. Dell had been sent
there from Cleveland in the expansion draft to play
for the newly formed Hornets.

Four years passed. The Currys were closer to
family and it just felt right to be here. Sonya and
Dell had expanded their own family. Steph's little
brother Seth was three. And there was another
baby on the way.

One afternoon at their Charlotte home, Sonya
Curry couldn't help but marvel as she looked out
of her kitchen window watching five-year-old Steph
play on the plastic hoop in their driveway. Other
kids would do something for a while and then get
bored of it quickly and move on to something else.
Not little Steph. He would be at that little basket for
hours. He never got bored with it. Every chance he
got, he would be out there shooting baskets.

He's so small, Sonya thought, as Steph took another shot.

He was smaller and skinnier than most other kids his age, which was kind of funny since his dad was so big and tall. Steph couldn't even jump high enough to dunk the ball on the toy hoop. But that didn't stop him from trying.

She watched as he went to work on some longer shots. Steph, even at this young age, had discipline and dedication. A five-year-old with a work ethic. She beamed with pride. She loved watching him out there having the time of his life, doing something that he obviously loved to do.

Steph sank another shot and went back to the same spot over and over again to make sure he had it down right.

Sonya opened the kitchen window.

"Steph, it's time to stop playing and come in for dinner now," she said.

Steph stopped and stared at his mother with a look of disappointment that almost made her laugh. The boy would stay out playing at that hoop all night if she gave him half a chance. He'd never come in to eat or drink.

"C'mon now. You heard what I said. Maybe after dinner you can play a bit more."

Steph flashed a huge smile and rushed through the back door into the kitchen for dinner. He didn't care much about the food. All he could think of was how much fun it would be playing *after* dinner.

One Sunday morning Steph and Seth opened the car doors and began to run as fast as they could to the rickety basket attached to the utility pole in the backyard. Steph had a basketball tucked under his arm.

But before they had gotten three steps from the car they were intercepted by Grandma Duckie, who had her arms spread out wide like a net about to haul in a load of fish.

"Whoa, there!" Grandma Duckie cried.

Steph and Seth stopped abruptly and looked up at their grandmother, who now had her hands on her hips and was looking at them sternly.

"So you two boys were planning on running to

that basket before you say hello to your grandma and give her a big hug?" she said.

Steph and Seth looked down on the ground and shuffled their feet in the dirt.

"Sorry, Grandma," Steph said sheepishly. "We just…"

"Never you mind," Grandma Duckie said as her face erupted into a huge smile. "You can just give me that hug right now!"

Steph and Seth dove into Grandma Duckie's arms as she gathered them in. Steph thought she was going to squeeze the life out of him. But that was okay. He liked hugging his grandma and he liked coming to Grottoes, Virginia, where his father had grown up. It felt like his second home.

Grandma said, "You kind of remind me of somebody I know."

"Who?" Steph asked.

Grandma Duckie smiled. "Your dad. He spent night and day, rain and shine here playing ball. Once your grandfather put that old rim on that utility pole, we couldn't get him away from it. One summer his sisters were supposed to be watching him while me and your Grandpa were at work and they locked your daddy outside the house with nothing but a basketball and that hoop all day long."

"Wow," Steph said. "That's so cool!"

Dell laughed as he walked over to the boys from the car. "Your aunties would push me out in the morning and just slip a sandwich and a drink out the window at lunch. I'd eat and be at that old rim the rest of the afternoon. Then they'd let me back in and clean me up just before Grandma and Grandpa got home and swear me to secrecy!"

Dell winked at the boys. "But why would I tell on them?" he chuckled. "I was having the time of my life!"

Steph looked up at his father. "Is that really a true story?"

Dell rubbed Steph's head. "Sure is. Thanks to my sisters, I'm in the NBA today."

"Sounds like they were kind of mean," Steph replied.

Dell rolled his eyes. "Well, maybe a little, but I was just an annoying little brother in a house full of older sisters who just wanted to watch TV in peace. I ended up with a great jump shot, though."

Grandma Duckie looked at Dell and said, "Too bad your father isn't around to watch these two shooting baskets at that old rim like you used to."

Steph looked at his father and saw his smile turn to a look of sadness. Grandpa Jack had died when Steph was only three. He didn't remember much about him.

Dell sighed deeply and shook his head slowly. "Yep, Pops would have loved it."

Grandma Duckie looked at Seth and Steph and said, "Well, go on. What are you waiting for?"

The boys didn't need to be asked twice. They both sprinted to the utility pole, where the battered rim and backboard was waiting for them.

Steph immediately threw up a shot and it missed. The ball bounced back to the ground, rebounded off a rock in the dirt and then rolled into the woods.

"You know the rules," Seth laughed. "You have to go get it. Don't get eaten."

Steph sighed. He loved this old rim, but sometimes it could be a pain. At home, his half-

court had a nice level concrete surface to play on.
The backboard was NBA-quality glass. There was
even an NBA three-point line. It was surrounded by
a fence so he didn't have to run into the woods and
worry about getting eaten by bears or wolverines
when he needed to retrieve a missed shot.

He and Seth had it good compared to their dad
growing up. But, that was why his dad had gotten
so good. He had to learn the hard way. If he missed
a shot, he had to run after it, so he tried hard not
to miss shots. The rim was hard and unforgiving, so
he learned to put the ball in the hole with pinpoint
accuracy and a soft touch.

He took a deep breath and headed to the woods
to retrieve the ball.

"When I get back," he yelled over his shoulder,
"Let's play some one-on-one."

"Sure," Seth yelled. "Just don't cheat this time!"

Steph rolled his eyes as he looked up at the blue
Virginia sky. Seth always accused him of cheating.
Especially when he was losing a game. Steph didn't
even bother to reply. As he looked for the ball
hidden somewhere among the trees, he kept an

eye out the whole time. Not that he was afraid of getting eaten by a bear or wolverine. But it didn't hurt to be careful, just in case.

H-O-R-S-E

Steph was sure that this was his day.

As he dribbled the ball in Charlotte's Hornets Coliseum, he watched his father working on a shooting drill and wondered if they would have a chance to play H-O-R-S-E after practice today. It was fun to play against his dad at home, and he and his Pops played often there. But to get to play H-O-R-S-E surrounded by thousands of empty seats at the Charlotte Coliseum was kind of magical.

Steph knew he had it good. How many eight-year-old kids got to go to practices and take shots with a professional basketball team? How many kids got to play one-on-one against some of the best players in the world? Of course, he never won any of those games because his dad told his teammates not to give him a break just because he was a kid.

"Don't go easy on him!" Dell would bark with a slight grin on his face.

As long as he could remember, he had been going to his Dad's practices. When he was little, Steph pestered his Pops to let him tag along. Dell finally asked Coach Bristow if it was okay if Steph could come. When the coach said yes, Steph couldn't wait to be part of it, to take it all in.

He and Seth played hide-and-seek in the huge arena. The staff all knew him and his brother and would offer them snacks and ice cream cones.

When the players took a water break, he would rush on to the court to shoot some hoops. When the team broke into half-court drills, Steph would be on the other half of the court shooting. If Seth was at the practice, they would get into a heated one-on-one game on the other half, which always seemed to have at least one moment when Seth would shout at Steph, "You're cheating!" if he was behind in the game.

But most importantly, Steph watched the players to see how it was done.

Steph felt like he was the luckiest kid in the world. He was seeing what went on behind the scenes. He got to witness how professional basketball players worked day in day out.

His mother always told him, "Watch your Father. Watch how he does it." And he did watch him. He watched him during practices and he watched him when he got to go to home Hornet games—when it wasn't a school night, of course. His mom was a stickler about his studies and made it no secret that those came first. After all, she was the head and founder of the school he attended—Charlotte Montessori School–Lake Norman.

He filed away what he saw. He learned that what you did when you didn't have the ball in your hands was just as important as what you did when it was in your hands. Basketball wasn't just about shooting; it was about ball handling and defense and being aware of where your teammates were and what the defense might do.

He watched the drills during practices. What did they work on? What were the tricks and skills that he needed to be competitive? He didn't just learn from his Dad; he learned from the other players on the Hornets. He knew all the players and they knew him. He and Seth were unofficial mascots of the Hornets.

Steph watched center Vlade Divac, who at 7'1" might as well have been a skyscraper with a beard, muscle his way to the rim. He analyzed Glen Rice's moves as he drove to the basket and soft touched a jumper into the hoop from three feet out. But out of all the players on his Pop's team, he always kept the closest eye on Muggsy Bogues.

He was something special.

Muggsy wasn't only small on the court, but he was small in real life, too. At 5'3" he was the smallest professional basketball player in the NBA. He was the smallest player who had EVER played in the NBA.

Steph shook his head as he watched Muggsy work on a ball handling drill. Muggsy was shorter than some of the kids Steph played against in his kid's rec league. And yet, here he was, moving effortlessly and confidently among NBA giants.

Muggsy was lightning fast and he dribbled the

ball like he was born with one in his hands. As the team's point guard, he instinctively knew where his players were going to be and when to fire off a perfect pass to the open man. Muggsy didn't score as much as Steph's father did, but Muggsy was the man who made those points possible. He was tiny, but he ran the team.

Steph was impressed.

Muggsy saw Steph staring at him. He stopped the drill he was working on and ran over and grabbed Steph, lifted him up on his shoulder and started running around the top of the key with him. Steph started yelling while the other members of the Hornets laughed.

Muggsy finally put him down and put his hands on Steph's shoulders.

"Well, little man," Muggsy said, appraising Stephen. "It looks like you got taller. Pretty soon you're going to be taller than me, although that ain't saying much."

Stephen smiled and nodded. Sometimes it felt like that would never happen. Kids made fun of him because he was so small. How would he ever be able to play in the NBA someday if he didn't get bigger and stronger? Sometimes he wondered if he would ever be as good as his Dad or Muggsy.

Muggsy sensed what was going through Stephen's mind and looked him straight in the eye.

"Now what did I tell you about size?" he asked.

Stephen looked down and said softly, "It's not the size of the man—it's the size of his heart that matters."

"That's straight talk, little man," Muggsy said seriously. "When I was a kid, nobody took me seriously when I stepped on the court. But that lit the fire in me. Made me want to work harder to prove them wrong. They underestimated me at their own peril. I see the same thing in you. You're a fighter."

Steph smiled. "You think so?"

Muggsy put his arm around Steph's shoulder. "I know so. I also know that you got that look in your eye."

"What look?"

"Like you're gonna challenge your pops to a game of H-O-R-S-E today."

"Are you a mind reader now?" Stephen laughed.

Muggsy winked. "I'm part Leprechaun. Why do you think I'm so small?"

They laughed as Muggsy grabbed a ball, dribbled hard to the basket, and dunked it with a resounding slap. He turned and faced Steph. "Like I said, size of the heart."

He winked at Steph and then said, "Size of the jump doesn't hurt either."

Steph shook his head and laughed as he dribbled the ball at the top of the key.

It was true. He had been practicing extra hard at home so he would be ready to challenge his Dad. He had been working on his long ball and his dribbling and his reverse layups so much that he was sure the neighbors were getting tired of hearing the thump, thump, thump of the basketball on the family court. He knew that he had to work on his game, day in and day out if he was ever going to beat his Pops at H-O-R-S-E.

His Dad told him that you play to win. And his father *never* let him win. He didn't do it in a mean way. He didn't taunt him or gloat after the wins, but he made it known that he was not going to hand Steph a charity victory just because he was a kid. His Pops taught him that you have to earn your victories in life and in sports—and you did that through hard work and practice.

Steph watched as the practice ended and the players started making their way to the locker room. It was time to get down to business.

Steph dribbled next to his Dad and said, "Hey, Pops, you up for a game of H-O-R-S-E before we go home?"

Dell looked down at Steph and smiled. "Always. I'll even let you take first shot."

Steph didn't hesitate. He dribbled to the free throw line, stopped and threw up the shot from his hip. Steph had been working on his accuracy, but he still didn't really have a jump shot. He needed to heft the ball from down low just to get the ball to the rim.

Swish!

Dell grabbed a ball and repeated what Steph had done. And he missed! The ball bounced off the heel of the rim and went high into the air.

"That's H for you," Steph said jubilantly. *This is my day! I knew it!*

The battle went back and forth with layups and shots off the glass, reverse layups, shots from the side and shots near the rim, hits and misses. Dell finished the game with a shot from the top of the key that Steph didn't quite have the strength enough to heft to the rim. His ball hit the front of the rim and careened forward back to Steph.

The result was Dell: H-O; Steph: H-O-R-S-E.

Dell put his arm around Steph and said, "Good game. Your shots are getting more consistent. Now here's what you might think about..." and he spent the next several minutes analyzing Steph's form and suggesting how he might improve it.

Steph had lost again. But he wasn't upset. Well maybe just a little. He had learned since the very beginning of playing H-O-R-S-E with his Dad that getting upset and crying didn't do any good if he wanted to improve his game. He would still have the loss and he wouldn't have learned anything.

Muggsy had hung around to watch them play. He had a huge smile on his face. Steph looked over and made eye contact with him. Muggsy thumped his heart with his fist and pointed back to Steph.

Steph smiled briefly as his father put his arm around his shoulder and they started to leave the court.

Size of your heart, Steph thought. *Size of your heart.*

Backyard Boot Camp

STEPH WAS NOT HAVING FUN. His parents had never forced any sports on him. But once he did decide to commit to a sport, it was expected that he would give his all, for himself and for his teammates.

That is what Currys did.

He had tried different sports. Steph liked baseball and was pretty good at it. Last year he had played on a state champion-winning youth baseball team. Baseball was fun.

He also loved golf. When his Dad took him on the golf course when he was little, he had immediately been bitten by the golf bug. He had even seriously considered concentrating on golf as his sport of choice. He loved playing it and marveled when he watched the top pros making impossible shots on television. But, he knew deep down, that the sport he really loved was basketball. It had always been basketball.

Basketball flowed in his veins. It was the heartbeat that kept him going.

And right now, his heart was racing.

He was going through a boot camp in their backyard.

And his mother was his drill instructor.

"C'mon, Steph," Sonya said firmly. "I need 10 more platform leaps without resting. Go!"

Sweat was running down his forehead and stinging his eyes. He closed his eyes, said a brief prayer, then leapt on to the platform and jumped down. Leapt up and jumped down. Ten times in succession; his mother shouting encouragement the whole time.

If only he had chosen golf over basketball. He was pretty sure that golfers didn't do platform leaps and lunges, and lunges with hops and pushups, and pushups with pop ups, and jumping jack planks, and skater jumps, and mountain climbers and squats, and squats with jump ups and...

His mother called it Plyometrics.

Steph called it Hell on Earth.

Right about now, his friends' mothers were

probably making them snacks or bringing them cool drinks. He was pretty sure that the other mothers weren't running backyard boot camps and torturing their 11-year-old children to improve their agility and leaping abilities.

But most kids didn't have mothers who had been elite volleyball players at Virginia Tech, either. It was cool, because that is where his mom had met his dad. And his mom was every as bit competitive as his dad—maybe more.

At the end of the last jump down, he bent over, hands on his knees. His legs were on fire and he was breathing so hard he thought his lungs were going to explode out of his chest. His mother had told him that these exercises would help him improve his game. Deep down, he thought she was right and it might help him in the long run—if it didn't kill him first.

Steph straightened up slowly and raised his hand. "Can I rest for 10 minutes?" he asked.

Sonya put her hands on her hips, a look of irritation on her face. "Are you going to tell that to an opponent you're guarding? Hold on. I'm tired?"

Stephen nodded no, but he felt like he was going to start crying.

Sonya sensed this and her face softened. She walked over and put her arm around Steph's shoulder. "Look, Steph, I know it's hard. Most things you really want are. When I was playing volleyball at Virginia Tech, there were times I got so tired and frustrated, I just wanted to walk away. But in the end, I knew I loved the game and I just wanted to be as good as I could be."

Steph looked at the ground, still breathing hard.

Sonya continued, "Let's face it. You've never been the biggest or the fastest kid on the court. But you make up for that in head and heart. I know you love the game, but if you want to compete, you are going to have to work harder than the other kids. It's about commitment to the game and to yourself."

Sonya rubbed Steph's head and he smiled.

"And that commitment begins right now," Sonya said seriously. "So I'll need some lunges from you. It'll help strengthen your legs and your core. Let's go."

The smile left Stephen's face as quickly it had appeared. He looked at his mother and could tell she wasn't kidding. Pep talk over. It was time to get to work. He took his first lunge and winced. It felt like his leg was going to fall off.

His mom said they were going to do this every day for two weeks to prep for his middle school basketball practices. *Just two more weeks,* he thought, as he did another painful lunge. *I hope I live to tell about it.*

When Steph woke up it was still dark outside, but he couldn't help it. He was super excited. He had worked so hard and he felt like he was ready. His mother had already put him through endurance drills, and he had practiced with intense focus. And now it was finally here: the first basketball game of the season for the Charlotte Christian Knight middle school team and he couldn't wait to suit up and get on to the court to play.

He dressed hurriedly and ran to the kitchen to grab breakfast, making sure that he had his jersey and his shoes tucked into in his red, white, and blue athletic backpack. When he got to the kitchen, his mother was waiting for him, her arms crossed, leaning against the sink and not looking happy. Seth and Sydel were already at the table eating breakfast. Seth was avoiding making eye contact with him.

Uh, oh.

Steph stopped dead in his tracks.

"So, Wardell Stephen Curry," Sonya said to him quietly, but forcefully.

When she called him Wardell Stephen Curry, he knew he was in trouble. But he couldn't figure out what he had done. What was it? Then suddenly, like a bolt of lightning, it hit him: *the dishes.*

It wasn't many dishes, only about four or five, but his mother had told him to do them last night. Instead, he went outside for an hour or so to work on his shooting so he'd be ready for the game today. He figured it wouldn't be a big deal if he just fudged a little on the dishes.

He realized that probably wasn't such a great idea. His mom was a stickler about the chores. And she was all about responsibility and owning up to the consequences of your actions. But it was only a few dishes. He knew she was upset about it, but it seemed like such a minor thing.

"You know I asked you to do the dishes last night and yet here I see them still in the sink," Sonya said sternly.

"I'm sorry," he answered quietly.

Sonya's stare bored into Stephen. "Sorry doesn't change the fact that you didn't do them. So I suggest that you get over to the sink right now."

Stephen didn't smile as he looked at his mother, but he was relieved. Just do the dishes he hadn't done last night? That wasn't so bad. He felt like he had just dodged a very large bullet.

As he put his backpack down near the table and headed toward the sink, Sonya continued, "And you will not be playing in your game today."

Steph stopped and stared at his mother in disbelief.

"What?" he said incredulously.

"You heard me," Sonya said. "You will tell your coach and your teammates that you won't be playing in today's game and you will tell them why you won't be playing. If your coach has any questions he can call me."

"But Mom," Steph cried. "It's our first game today! It was only a few dishes. That isn't fair!"

Sonya straightened up and put her hands on her hips. "You had a family obligation and you didn't meet it. I saw you practicing in the back yard yesterday evening instead of doing the dishes. That was your choice and you made it. Now own up to the consequences."

"But what will I tell the team? What will I tell the coach?" Steph said with frustration in his voice, tears starting to well in his eyes.

"I suggest you tell your team and your coach the truth," Sonya said. "And I suggest that you get those dishes done. Playing basketball in this family is a privilege, not a God-given right. You need to get your priorities straight, young man."

All Steph knew was that he felt awful and that a morning that had begun with excitement suddenly was filled with disappointment and anger. He sighed deeply, resigned. With tears in his eyes, he walked slowly to the kitchen sink and began washing the dishes.

Toronto

"WE'RE MOVING TO TORONTO?" Steph said, a little shocked. "For how long?"

"Will it be forever?" Seth cried. "What about my friends?"

Sonya raised her hand. "No. Not forever. Just for the season. We decided that it would be good to be closer to your father for a while. He misses us and we are all missing him."

Steph nodded. That was true. The last couple of years had been hard on everybody since his Dad was away so much during the season.

He did miss his Pops. A lot.

But he couldn't help but think, *Why did the Hornets trade my dad and wreck everything?*

After ten years with the Charlotte Hornets, his Pops had been traded to the Milwaukee Bucs and then the Bucs had traded him to the Toronto Raptors. His dad had been with the Raptors for two years now. The first warning sign was when

Muggsy Bogues was traded to the Golden State Warriors. Charlotte loved Muggsy as much as it loved his father, but that hadn't made any difference. It made Steph sad when Muggsy left.

And then his Dad was traded. But the Currys still stayed in Charlotte. Steph loved Charlotte. It was the only home he had ever really known. His friends were here, and his school and his home and his church. Charlotte flowed in his veins and now they were moving away to Canada?

Dell said quietly, "I know it'll be tough for everybody. But it will be fun, too. You guys can hang with me at Raptors practices more and do shoot arounds before games. Just like the old days." Dell nudged Steph with his elbow. "They also have a lot of good golf courses up there."

Steph looked down, but couldn't help but smile a little bit.

Steph and Seth looked at each other. Sydel was still young, she was only six, so it wasn't quite sinking in with her. She was looking at Steph and Seth to see if she should be upset about the news.

"We found this really nice condo overlooking Lake Ontario," Dell said. "We'll be able to rent a boat and even go fishing like me and my Pops used to do when he had some free time!"

"Ewww." The look of disgust on Sydel's face made everybody laugh.

Steph knew that it would be tough to go to a new school and make new friends. He was supposed to start 8th grade at Charlotte Christian this year. Steph was the star on his team by now, and he had been looking forward to playing with Seth this year.

"Where are we going to go to school?" Seth asked.

Sonya smiled at Seth briefly and said, "It's called Queensway Christian College."

"College!" Seth cried in alarm. "I can't go to college. I'm just starting middle school!"

Sonya chuckled. "No that's just what the school is called."

"Do they have a basketball team?" Steph asked.

Dell looked at Steph and shook his head. "Nope. They only have a hockey team. But don't worry.

We're going to buy you skates and sticks and everything."

Steph and Seth looked at each other with their mouths open.

Dell let out a loud laugh that startled Sydel. "Got ya!" he said, pointing at the boys. "Of course they have a basketball team!"

Steph laughed and pointed back at his dad. "Good one, Pops. You had me going for a second there."

Well, at least they had a basketball team and he'd be able to go to his Dad's practices.

"Do you know if their team is any good?" Steph said seriously.

Dell shook his head slowly. "Don't know about that. How bad could they be?"

How bad could they be, Steph thought. It was a question that would be answered soon enough when the family left Charlotte to the unknown adventure of living in a foreign country.

"Coach!"

James Lackey looked up and saw another of his

players holding his hands to his face. He shook his head and sighed as he walked over to the player, who was in obvious pain. Steph was with the boy, arms around his shoulder, trying to console him.

"Man, I am so sorry," Steph said to his teammate who was moaning. "I thought you were looking for the pass."

The teammate held up a hand and waved to Steph as if it was okay. But to Steph, it was not okay. This had been the third player in practice today who had to go to the sidelines because he had been hit in the head or face with an unexpected pass.

"Sorry, Coach, I thought he would be looking for the pass," Steph said as Coach Lackey approached.

"It's okay, Steph," the coach answered for the third time today.

But Steph felt bad. He was just trying to involve his teammates in the play. He never wanted to be accused of being a ball hog and he certainly wasn't trying to hurt them.

As Coach Lackey led the injured boy off the court, Steph remembered what his father had said before they came to live in Toronto. *How bad could they be?*

After his first practice with the team, he pretty much had his answer. While the Queensway College Saints basketball team wasn't exactly awful, nobody could accuse them of being amazingly good either. He should have had a clue when Coach Lackey introduced himself to Steph and Seth on the first day of school.

They had been sitting in the school office waiting for some paperwork to be completed so they could go to their first class. Suddenly, a stranger with dark, short-cropped hair burst into the office, looked around and directed his stare at Steph and Seth.

"Are you the Curry brothers? Steph and Seth?" he asked quickly.

At first Steph thought they might be in trouble or something, but the stranger was smiling as he approached. Steph nodded yes, avoiding eye contact. The man walked over briskly to where they were sitting and introduced himself. James Lackey. Coach of the middle school and senior high school basketball teams and history teacher. Big fan of their Dad.

The look on his face had been filled with excitement until Steph stood up to shake his hand. All 5'4" of him. The expression on his face went to surprise in a millisecond. It had been a quick look and Coach Lackey had done a good job of covering it up, but Steph recognized it all too well.

The Coach had been expecting the monster son of an NBA player who could throw down dunks in his sleep. Instead he was shaking hands with a short, skinny kid who looked like he should be in 6th grade, not 8th grade. How could this kid possibly have game?

There was no sense in being angry. If Steph got angry every time somebody underestimated him because of the way he looked, he would be angry and discouraged all of the time.

Instead, he looked the coach in the eye, smiled widely and said, "Glad to meet you, Coach! When are tryouts for the team?"

"No tryouts. Just show up for practice and you're on the team!" said the coach.

Just show up and you're on the team? Steph immediately had a bad feeling about that.

Kind of for good reason, it turned out.

Practice had come to a halt as Coach Lackey attended to Steph's fallen teammate on the sideline. He spoke to the player, gave him an icepack for his forehead and then made his way back to Steph, who was looking down at the court, hands on his hips, feeling badly.

Coach Lackey said quietly, "You might need to dial it down a bit until your teammates catch up with you a bit more. They aren't used to playing with somebody as good as you. Heck, I'm not used to coaching somebody as good as you. You could be starting for our high school team."

Steph nodded seriously. "Got it, Coach," he said.

"Okay," Coach Lackey chuckled. "Let's see if we can get through the rest of the practice without another casualty."

The coach blew his whistle to resume practice, watching in awe as Steph dribbled the ball down the court.

Just Give Me the Ball

THE SAINTS WERE IN A SITUATION that they hadn't been in all year and Coach Lackey was out of ideas. Usually, at this point in a game, they were well ahead and he didn't have to worry about the outcome. They had blown out everybody that they had faced, thanks to Steph Curry.

Steph had usually scored 40 or 50 points, making at least a few miraculously impossible shots that wowed the crowd along the way, and the game was in the bag. It had gone that way all season. But now it looked like their undefeated season was about to be a thing of the past.

They were down by 8 points against Hillcrest Jr. Public School with a minute left in the game.

The Saints had waltzed through the Mentor College Tournament and found themselves facing a Hillcrest team with several players over 6 feet tall. Hillcrest had harassed Stephen the whole game.

They double and triple teamed him. They dared him to drive into the lane against their much taller players.

"Where's your dad, now?" one of their players hissed in his ear.

Coach Lackey called a time out to regroup. As the players gathered around him, Lackey had little inspiration to offer them. "Guys, I think the only thing we can do is try harder."

The whole team looked stunned and said nothing. The coach had run out of ideas and no one seemed to have any better suggestions.

And then Steph spoke.

"Give me the ball," he said quietly.

"What?" Coach Lackey said, not sure if he had heard Steph correctly.

"Just give me the ball and we'll win," he said.

Lackey had learned to never underestimate what Steph Curry could do, and he saw little reason to doubt that now.

Lackey just shrugged and said, "Okay, just give Steph the ball and get out of his way."

Nobody argued.

Anticipating that Steph would be the go-to on the inbound pass, Hillcrest's defense lined up high to stop a possible three. Seeing that they were lining high, Steph dribbled the ball two steps and simply pulled up two feet in front of them and fired a shot before they had time to react.

Swish!

As Hillcrest brought the ball down court, Steph picked off an errant pass and dribbled up court. He didn't hesitate and let loose a long ball that was two feet farther from the basket than his previous shot. It went up so high it seemed to take forever before it arced back down to the rim. The crowd held its breath.

Swish!

The gym erupted. Two quick threes in 15 seconds. The Saints were suddenly down by only two points with 30 seconds left on the clock. The impossible suddenly seemed possible.

The swagger that Hillcrest had shown all game disappeared. The players had worried looks on their faces as they brought the ball down court and took an ill-advised three to try to ice the game. It missed and the Saints rushed the ball back up court, passing the ball to Steph high on their own side. This time, two Hillcrest players ran out to defend him, but Steph, seeing wide-open teammate Casey Field above the three line, flicked a quick pass to him.

It was as if Steph had not only passed the basketball to Casey, but had also passed along his will and determination over to his teammate. Casey didn't hesitate for a moment and put the ball up.

Swish!

The people in the crowd were now up on their feet, jumping up and down. The screams were deafening as the Saints took a one-point lead.

Hillcrest was suddenly in panic mode. What had just happened? Time had been on their side half a minute ago, but now they found themselves down by a point with only twenty seconds to play. They took the ball down court, looking for a good open shot and it looked like they had one, but the shot missed and the Saints rebounded. Once again, Stephen was given the ball. He dribbled to the three-point line, hesitated, and then pretended like he was going to penetrate by taking a quick step forward. When the two defenders on him took the bait and began to collapse into the middle of the key to cut him off, Steph saw his opportunity.

It was a millisecond, but that was all he needed. The two defenders watched helplessly as Steph stepped back instantly and fired another long three. He didn't even need to watch the shot go into the hole. He ran back to get into a defensive position as the ball hit the net.

The crowd couldn't believe it. Coach Lackey stood on the sidelines with his mouth open. An eight-point deficit had been erased and had become a four-point lead in less than one minute. It was insane, but he was convinced now that nothing was impossible when Steph Curry had the ball.

As the final buzzer sounded, Steph looked up at the scoreboard. Somehow, against all odds, the Saints had won by six points. Briefly, he lowered his head and said a prayer. It had been an impossible victory, but it hadn't entirely surprised Steph. He knew that he couldn't have done it without his teammates.

It was the story of David and Goliath he heard at home and in church. He was convinced that miracles happen every day. You just have to believe.

When he finally looked up, a human tidal wave of ecstatic parents and teammates were heading his way.

Varsity Blues

AT THE END OF HIS THIRD SEASON with the Raptors, Steph's Dad decided to call it quits. The family had spent only one season living in Toronto. Dell told them that after 16 years in the NBA it was time to do other things. Steph was going to start high school and Dell wanted to help coach him and to be there for his games.

They were going back home to Charlotte.

Steph had mixed feelings about his Dad's retirement.

On the one hand, it was going to be great having Dad around more, helping him develop his game. Maybe he would get good enough to play at Virginia Tech like his Pops. That was the dream.

On the other hand, he would miss hanging out with his father at practices and doing shoot arounds before games. He would miss the games of H-O-R-S-E in the empty arenas after practices and

the one-on-one games against NBA stars. He would
even miss Toronto. He would miss the Canadian
candy—especially the Maynard's Fuzzy Peaches.

He was excited to be back at home and to enroll
at Christian for his freshman year of high school.
All the pieces were falling into place. He thought
he might even have a shot at making the varsity
basketball team. He had tried out for the varsity
squad and played hard and he felt he was ready.

But Shonn Brown, the head coach of the
Charlotte Christian Knights varsity squad, had a
different idea.

"Look, Steph, I think you are a skilled player,
but I don't think you are ready to play varsity yet,"
Coach Brown said evenly when they met one
evening at his office.

Steph looked directly at the coach. This meant
that instead of playing against tougher competition,
he would be playing junior varsity for at least this
season. Not the end of the world, but still not
entirely what he wanted to hear, either.

"You need to work on your strength, speed,

and defense," Coach Brown continued. "You'll get your chance, and I'm sure you'll have a productive varsity career. You just need a little more time to develop."

Time to develop, Steph thought. What the coach had said without saying it was that he thought Steph was still too small to play varsity. And he was the smallest kid on the court. He was only 5'6" and skinny and he was going against much larger and stronger juniors and seniors. On the other hand, he had been playing one-on-one games against real men—NBA professionals—since he was kid. He grew up with the best teachers in the world.

Yet Coach Brown had some valid points. He wasn't as strong as some of the bigger, more athletic players. He still had to bring the ball up from his hip to make his threes because he wasn't strong enough to hoist a more traditional jump shot. And there were a lot of upper classmen who had worked hard to make the varsity squad.

Steph could understand all of that.

But he couldn't help but wish he would grow so people wouldn't be so quick to judge him.

It seemed that almost everyone—coaches, parents, opposing players—took one look at him and made up their minds: he was too small; he was too soft; he looked like a baby compared to the other kids.

Every time he moved up an age bracket, the questions always were, "How old is that kid? What's he doing here? That's Dell Curry's son?"

And each time he stepped on the court he had to prove himself. Over the years he had developed a chip on his shoulder about it. Short, skinny as a toothpick Steph Curry had to work twice as hard for every inch of territory he gained, and he enjoyed showing kids and parents that he belonged.

Muggsy Bogues had told him when he was a kid that it wasn't the size of the man, but the size of his heart that mattered. But, right now, it felt like his heart was breaking.

Steph lowered his head, trying to mask his disappointment as Coach Brown continued talking. He was a good coach and maybe it was for the best. His mother was always telling him that when God closes a door, he opens a window.

"So, Steph," Coach Brown concluded. "Work hard at JV this year and we'll see how it goes. I'm sure you'll do great things there."

Steph nodded and smiled weakly. "Sure, Coach," he replied.

Time to put in the work, Steph thought.

He turned around and began walking to the gym exit. It seemed like it took forever before he finally reached the door.

Give Him the Keys

THINGS WEREN'T GOING WELL for Charlotte Christian Knights basketball team.

Coach Brown had pulled out all the stops against Ravenscroft School in the state playoff tournament game and his team still couldn't seem to make up ground against tough and talented Ravenscroft.

They needed a spark and he thought maybe that spark was just a few players away from him near the end of the bench. He looked down at Steph Curry, who as usual, was intensely focused on what was happening on the court. It wasn't unusual for a coach to call up a talented JV player to play with the varsity team during the playoffs—and calling up Steph had been a no-brainer.

He had simply ruled the court at the JV level. Every time he had a chance to watch Steph practice or play in games, Brown had found that the quiet and respectful kid had brought something new to

his game that he hadn't seen before. Curry's game
IQ was growing faster than the boy's body.

"Curry," Coach Brown called loudly as he
gestured to Steph. "Over here."

Steph looked over and hesitated for a moment,
pointing to himself, surprised as if saying, "Me?"

Coach Brown nodded, hurriedly gesturing with
his hands.

Steph stood up, walked over to Coach Brown
and got down on one knee, busily chewing on his
jagged mouthpiece.

"Check in at the scorer's table. You're going in.
Try to make something happen," Coach Brown said
evenly.

Steph's heart leapt a little. He was actually going
to see action in a playoff game? As a freshman? It
was an honor to be called up for the playoffs, but
usually called-up JV players practiced with varsity,
suited up for the games, and then sat on the bench
the entire time, supporting the team with their
voices; more glorified cheerleaders than players.

But he had practiced with the varsity as if he
was going to play every minute of every playoff

game. He sat in on team video sessions, studying opposition players as if he was going to start. He thought about the upcoming games at night before he went to sleep.

Suddenly the buzzer sounded and he found himself on the court.

As soon as he stepped foot on the boards, he could hear the laughter coming from the Ravenscroft side.

"Towel boy!" somebody yelled as a section of the crowd erupted.

"Are you lost, little boy?" another chimed in.

Steph chewed on his ragged mouthpiece as he listened to the taunts, but this was no time to listen to that. Besides, his mother was drowning out the taunts. He could hear her cheering at the top of her lungs, "You go, Steph!"

Steph smiled a little. Always there to support him. That is, when she wasn't yelling at him from the stands to play tougher defense.

It didn't make any difference. He'd heard it all before. He had been put into the game and he had a job to do. Everything became very quiet in his mind and the only thing that mattered was what was in front of him on the court.

He didn't feel in over his head. He had put in the work. He was ready for this.

Steph received the inbound pass and quickly brought the ball up court. His mind started firing as he looked for potential open teammates to pass off to as he dribbled up.

The Ravenscroft players had a tendency to run back on defense quickly. Too quickly. They were playing a tough zone, choking off the middle and the post, but they weren't coming out far enough to defend the three. Steph had been seeing it all game. It was obvious they had no respect for Charlotte Christian's outside game.

Suddenly, being a freshman JV call-up had its advantages. He could tell they had no respect for him. After all, he was just a 12-year-old water boy thrown into the game.

But Steph knew better.

The Ravenscroft players were sure he was going to pass the ball off. They were sure that he would be afraid to pull the trigger. He could visualize how the defenders were going to react as he got closer to the three-point line. They had underestimated him and now he was going to make them pay for it.

As he rushed to the line, the defenders did exactly what Steph had thought they would do. They sat waiting for him to move in closer, anticipating that he was going to penetrate and then pass the ball off. Instead, Steph simply pulled up and let loose a three-point attempt from above the top of the key.

He could see from the surprised look in the defender's eyes that he caught him completely off guard. He watched helplessly as Steph's ball arced high and dropped through the hoop with nothing but a quiet swishing sound.

The Ravenscroft players weren't the only surprised people in the gym.

Although Coach Brown balled his fist and shouted "Yes!" after Steph scored, he hadn't seen that coming at all.

He had to admit, the kid had some ice in his veins. He had thrown him into a situation that would have intimidated most freshmen and he had just calmly thrown down a three in a pressure-packed playoff game as if it was nothing at all. Steph didn't jump up and down after the basket. He simply went back to work on defense.

It was as if Coach Brown had suddenly seen the future in the skinny, too-short kid who he thought hadn't been ready for varsity a few short months ago. He shook his head, turned to an assistant and said softly, "We need to hand him the keys to our program."

Charlotte Christian was eliminated from the playoffs in an 11-point loss to Ravenscroft, but as the disappointed team sat in the darkened bus for the long ride home, Coach Brown wasn't completely discouraged. He was certain that the future of his basketball program was looking bright.

He glanced at Steph who was deep in thought.

Basketball mind still at work, Coach Brown thought as the bus drove into the night.

Growing Pains

Steph was distracted.

He was trying to pay attention to what the youth pastor was saying to the Central Church of God youth group, but he kept looking over at Ayesha Alexander.

He felt a little guilty about it, but that didn't stop him. She had joined the youth group not that long ago and they had talked a little. He knew that she was 14 years old—a year younger than him— and that she had lived in Toronto for a while, just like him.

She seemed really nice but she was shy.

As the youth pastor continued to talk, he continued to look over at Ayesha.

Suddenly, her head turned and she stared directly at him! Steph felt his face getting hot and his stomach suddenly felt empty. *Look away! Look away now!*

It was as if Ayesha was thinking the same thing. Their eyes met briefly and then they hurriedly looked away, staring past each other as if they had actually been looking at something else.

Steph swallowed hard as he stared straight ahead in the direction of the youth pastor.

After the service, all the kids in the group got together and talked like they normally did. Steph tried to avoid Ayesha because he was embarrassed that he had gotten caught looking at her. It wasn't too hard to avoid her because it looked like she was trying to avoid him, too.

Steph stayed and talked to the pastor for a bit. After he said goodbye to the pastor, he noticed that everybody had left the room. All except for one person: Ayesha.

Steph could feel his heart pounding.

Ayesha didn't look mad as she approached him. In fact she kept looking up, then down, trying to avoid eye contact. Steph looked down and noticed she had something in her right hand.

Finally, she stopped two feet from him, raised her hand, and offered him what she was holding.

It was a package of Maynard's Fuzzy Peaches: his favorite Canadian candy of all time!

Steph took the candy from her, but couldn't get his mouth to work.

Finally, he blurted out, "Thanks!"

Ayesha looked at him, then looked down and then sideways. It looked like she wanted to say something, but couldn't get it out.

Then she hurriedly turned and practically ran out of the room, she was walking so fast. All Steph could do was watch her leave. It felt like his feet were frozen in place.

He looked down at the candy and then at the empty doorway. That was unexpected. If he was on the basketball court he would have known what to do, but girls were a far different thing than basketball. He thought that maybe he should try to get to know her a little bit better.

Someday.

The next day he was at the gym with his father.

"Try it again," Dell told Steph. Dell's voice echoed in the empty Charlotte Christian gym as a frustrated Steph took yet another pass from his father.

Dell and Steph both knew that this had been coming for a long time and had decided that the summer leading into Steph's junior year at Charlotte Christian would be the time when Steph's shot should be transformed.

And right now, Steph was hating it. Hating every second of it.

Steph took the basketball at shoulder height, dipped it down and then brought it up above his head, attempting to align his feet to the left so his right hip and his shooting arm could align to the basket. From there, he concentrated, keeping his feet on the ground, and then he jumped just as he released it to give him the momentum he would need to get the ball to the rim. He tried to do all of this quickly as he kept his eyes on the rim until the ball was released from his right hand with a four finger snap. Once it was gone, he focused his attention on the ball as it sailed to the hoop and... missed the rim completely.

Steph groaned as the ball bounced harmlessly to

the floor. What had once been his lights out shot was now lights out bad. He wasn't used to being this awful. It was like trying to learn to breathe again only this time he was trying to learn to breathe under water.

As Coach Shonn Brown had vowed, he had indeed given the keys to the Charlotte Christian Knights basketball program to Steph in his sophomore year and he had been up to the task. He had helped lead the Knights to a league championship and a run into the playoffs.

Steph's ball handling was superb, his playmaking at point was excellent, and his game IQ was amazing. Although he had mainly been a pass-first guard, he still managed to dazzle the crowd with seemingly impossible long-distance shots. What could possibly be wrong with his game? Dell, who volunteered as assistant coach for the team, felt that there was a problem with his son's shot. Steph still released his shot from the hip and could be easily blocked by faster, taller, and stronger defenders.

Both Dell and Steph had discussed changing his

form for years—as far back as middle school. They knew that for Steph to be a complete player who could compete at the next level, he needed a better jump shot with a release point above his head.

Dell gathered the ball from the shot that Steph had just missed and passed it quickly to him. "Again!" he barked. "This time a wider stance, knees in a bit more. It will give you a little more power."

Steph took the pass and then dropped the ball and put his head down. He wiped tears from his eyes. "I can't do this," he said to his father. "I can't even make a shot outside of the paint anymore. I'm getting worse, not better."

Dell could feel Steph's pain, but he also knew that he couldn't give in. He remembered how angry and frustrated he had gotten sometimes when *his* father had come storming out of the house in Grottoes to make him correct his shot. He had hated that too sometimes.

"And you will probably get worse before you get better, but that doesn't mean you give up," Dell said quietly.

Steph shook his head. "I know, I know. But ... I suck."

Dell had to laugh. "Yes and you will suck for a while until you understand the mechanics of the new shot. Then, once you get THAT down, you'll have to learn to do it on the dribble and then from a crossover and then off a screen. Then you'll need to learn to make it off-balance with two defenders in your face. You'll need to be able to do it when you pull up and from deep. You'll have to learn to release it quickly before a defender even knows what hit him. You'll have to do it without thinking. You will do it so much that you'll see it in your dreams."

"More like in my nightmares," Steph grumbled.

Dell chuckled. "Hey, it could be worse. Your mother could be standing where I am now."

Steph laughed, but he was worried. What if he didn't get it? What if he stayed terrible? They were taking a risk changing everything going into his junior year. That's when colleges started seriously looking to recruit high school players. Was he blowing it?

He had gone to a basketball camp not long after he and Pops had started working on his new form. While he was there, he overheard one player saying to another, "I thought that Curry guy was supposed to be good. What happened?"

It stung.

He always felt like he had to prove himself on the court and now the one thing he had been really good at, his dead-eye accurate shooting from distance, had been taken away. It felt like his shooting arm had been cut off and he was trying to grow a new one back. Slowly. Painfully. An inch at a time.

But he knew his dad was right. He needed to work harder. He had grown a bit taller, but he was still small and thin and not as athletically gifted as other players. That was a fact.

Steph took a deep breath and said, "Okay, I'm ready. Let's do this."

Dell smiled. "That's what I'm talking about! Tell you what: at the end of this drill we'll take a break so I can whup you at H-O-R-S-E again. But you can only take shots using the new mechanics. How does that sound?"

Steph smiled and groaned. "Should I just concede the game now?"

Dell shook his head slowly. "Currys don't concede."

Steph knew his father was right. Until he had it down, he would never give up.

Shoot

"UM," STEPH SAID as the rest of the team laughed.
"We couldn't have ordered a medium jersey?"

He looked at Coach Brown, who had just handed
out the new uniforms at the end of practice and
who was doing a very bad job at trying to stifle
a laugh. Charlotte Christian had ordered new
uniforms for the basketball squad and had failed
to order Steph a medium jersey. The school just
assumed the players were all large or extra-large.

He wasn't all that buff to begin with and now
he looked like he was wearing an oversized sheet
with the number 20 on it. He had to admit, it
did look funny.

"Sorry, Steph," Coach Brown said. "But you are
stuck with it. We can't order you another one."

"I mean, I was planning on filling out more
this season, but this is a little extreme..." Steph
chuckled and shrugged.

The rest of the team laughed again.

He was laughing, but he could almost hear the taunts from the stands that would surely come when he ran on to the court looking like a little kid wearing an adult uniform.

As the team headed to the locker room, Coach Brown put his hand on Steph's shoulder and said quietly, "Steph, a word, please?"

Steph nodded and waited for Coach Brown to speak as the rest of the team disappeared through the locker room doors. *What did Coach Brown want? Had he done something wrong?*

When they were finally alone, Coach Brown looked at Steph and said, "Steph, you have to get it out of your head that you are a pass-first point guard."

Steph was a bit confused. "What are you saying, Coach?"

Coach Brown looked Steph right in the eye. "You need to shoot more."

Steph hesitated, then replied, "Coach, I don't want the team thinking I'm selfish. I don't want to be that guy who guns it all the time. I hate that guy when I see him on other teams."

Coach Brown smiled and shook his head. "I get that, Steph. And I appreciate that you are thinking about your teammates. But let me put it to you another way," Coach Brown sighed and put his hands on Steph's shoulders. "For us to win games, you need to take more shots."

At the beginning of summer, Coach Brown hadn't been as sure about this strategy as he was now. Steph had still been working on his new jump shot and it had been pretty ugly. He knew what Steph and Dell were doing and he was in agreement with it, but in the back of his mind he was hoping that the jump shot rebuilding project wasn't going to blow up in all of their faces.

Luckily, it hadn't. But that didn't surprise him. Steph worked harder than any player he had ever coached.

Coach Brown thought about the time he got a phone call from an irate mother of one of the players who demanded to know what he had been teaching Steph about handling the ball that he hadn't bothered to share with her son.

"Why aren't you teaching my son how to do

that? How come my boy can't do that?" she asked angrily.

Coach Brown only laughed and said that he actually had nothing to do with it. Steph had learned all of that on his own with just plain hard work and practice. He was always the first to get to the gym and the last to leave.

He looked at Steph and could see the wheels turning behind his eyes. He was thinking about what it would mean for him to take more shots and how he would do it while still keeping his teammates engaged in the game. Always the basketball mind.

"You're an upper classman now. You need to lead the team," Coach Brown finally said.

"Are you sure, Coach? I feel a little weird about it," Steph said quietly.

"Yes, Steph. I'm sure. And believe me, your teammates will not resent it," Coach Brown answered.

"Okay," Steph nodded. "Sure."

With that, Steph turned around and headed to the locker room, his big jersey flopping comically on his slight body. As Coach Brown watched him leave, he shook his head. One of the best all-around high school basketball players in the area and possibly in the entire state of North Carolina and he had to beg him to take more shots. Most kids wouldn't hesitate to be the star. Most kids were craving to be the center of attention.

Coach Brown chuckled. Most kids weren't Steph Curry.

Bob McKillop watched Steph playing at a summer Las Vegas basketball tournament that featured some of the top high school talent in the nation. Steph was on a team that Dell was coaching and he was simply playing awful.

McKillop was head basketball coach of the Davidson Wildcats.

He had been following Steph Curry's high school career since he was a freshman at Charlotte Christian. Davidson was close, less than an hour north of Charlotte, so McKillop had a front row seat to watch Steph develop as a player.

But the two went back further than that. Steph

and McKillop's son, Brendan, had played on a championship baseball team seven years earlier.

McKillop liked Steph. The kid was quiet and respectful. Down to earth and grounded. He had his parents to thank for that.

Steph had stepped up his junior year and had led Charlotte Christian to another league championship and then into the playoffs. He had improved his shooting form and his ball handling was exceptional. He had made over 40 percent of his threes and had proven that he was a scoring force to be reckoned with.

McKillop was very interested in recruiting Steph Curry to play at Davidson.

And even though today Steph was playing terribly in front of a gym full of college recruiters, McKillop couldn't for the life of him figure out why nobody else seemed interested in him. Going into his senior year, not one Atlantic Coast Conference college had made him an offer to come play for them. Not even Virginia Tech, where Dell Curry had been a star guard and Steph's mother had been an outstanding volleyball player.

It was as if Steph was invisible.

Sometimes, McKillop thought, really good athletes become invisible because colleges become blinded by size and athleticism. Steph was only 6'0" and maybe 160 pounds. He looked like he was 14 years old. He simply didn't *look* like he would be able to hold his own on the Division I basketball stage filled with top-tier five-star recruits, so they looked past him like he didn't exist.

And as McKillop watched Steph struggle on the court, he knew what the other coaches and recruiters from those college basketball programs who were also sitting in the stands were seeing: a small, skinny kid in over his head playing and struggling against top talent. They were blinded. They didn't see potential.

But McKillop knew better.

His assistant coach, Jim Fox, who had been tasked with scouting many of Steph's Charlotte Christian games, was sitting next to him. He was shaking his head.

"This is not going well for Steph," Fox said, leaning into McKillop.

McKillop smiled.

During a timeout, McKillop pointed to Steph, who was listening to his Dad give instructions in the huddle.

"Look at that," McKillop said to Fox. "Yeah, he's been terrible all game, but look at his body language. He isn't moping. He's still listening, and he's encouraging his teammates. Even though he's playing lousy, he's not letting it get to him. He's moving on."

McKillop would take a thousand players like Stephen Curry before he took a five-star recruit with a bad attitude and poor work habits. His Davidson teams had been filled with players who had been ignored by the big programs. They were hard-working kids hungry to prove themselves. It was about character and what he saw in Steph Curry was character and inner strength. That was something that didn't show up on a stat sheet.

Trust. Commitment. Care.

Those were three words McKillop emphasized to all of his players. It was how you built a team. It was how you built your life. They were words he lived by. He knew that Steph would live those words if he was lucky enough to get him to sign on at Davidson.

Steph's team broke from the time out and a few minutes later he turned the ball over again. Coach McKillop shook his head and chuckled a bit. Steph might be invisible to other coaches, but McKillop saw him. And he still liked what he saw.

After the game Steph was devastated.

He looked down, shaking his head as he sat on the hotel room bed, wondering why he had picked today of all days to have a simply awful game. There had been lot of Division I college basketball coaches and scouts at the gym and he had put in one of the worst performances of his life.

"I blew it, didn't I?" he said to his mother Sonya who was in the room with him. "I just totally blew it."

Sonya thought her heart was going to break. What could she say? He *had* been terrible. But he was her son and she didn't like to see him hurting so badly. And she also believed that things happen for a reason. She had faith that God had a plan for everyone.

Sonya walked over and hugged Steph briefly. She put her hands on his shoulders and said, "I'm not going to lie, you've had better games. But, listen to me: there are coaches out there who look for other things besides mind-blowing statistics. They look for character and composure. You were awful, but you didn't lose your head on the court today. People noticed that. I guarantee it."

Steph just shook his head slowly. "I don't know about that, Mom," he said quietly.

"I'm positive," Sonya said clearly. "Good coaches know that everybody has bad days. The ones who look beyond the bad days are the ones you want to play for."

"But I really needed to have a *good* day today. It was important," Steph said. "Maybe I should have played more AAU ball. Something."

She looked down at her son and smiled. "This day is done. You can't look forward when you're looking behind, am I right?"

Steph couldn't help but smile a little. His mom

was right. She always put things in perspective for him. There would be other days and he would work harder to make those days better.

He stood up and hugged his mother. "Thanks, Mom."

"Now, let's go meet your father to get something to eat," Sonya said evenly.

Steph nodded and smiled as the two left the hotel room and walked together into the bright desert sunshine of a new day.

I Want to Play

"So, Coach, you're saying there are no scholarships available at Virginia Tech?" Steph asked Seth Greenberg, the head coach of Virginia Tech's basketball team.

Coach Greenberg cleared his throat and shifted uncomfortably in his chair. Dell and Steph were sitting in front of his desk in his office and were waiting for an answer and he knew it was not going to sit well with them.

"We had several early commits," Coach Greenberg said slowly. "So yes, we have no more scholarships to give out. What I'm suggesting is that you walk-on and red shirt your freshman year. You won't play, but if you work hard, I'm pretty sure we will find you a scholarship for the next four years."

"Walk-on? And, I'd have to red shirt? Sit out a year?" Steph said, trying to hide his disappointment.

"Yes. Unfortunately, that's the best we can do," Greenberg shrugged.

Steph grew quiet. He wanted to play in college. Not be part of the practice squad.

Dell waited for a moment and then said, "Are you sure that is the best VT can do?"

"Sorry, Dell. That's the offer," Coach Greenberg said as he held his hands apart in a conciliatory gesture.

"Well, thank you, Coach," Dell said. "I'm sure that we'll need some time to think about this. We'll get back to you. Thank you for your time."

Both Dell and Stephen stood up, shook Coach Greenberg's hand, and left his office. Dell didn't need to be led out. He knew Virginia Tech like the back of his hand.

As they walked to the athletic department parking lot in the crisp autumn air, Steph could tell his father was not happy. Steph wasn't happy himself. It had been his lifelong dream to play at Virginia Tech.

Had Virginia Tech only come to scout his games because Dell Curry was a Hokie basketball legend and they figured they owed it to him? They were throwing Steph a bone and not a big one at that.

The Virginia Tech signing day he had imagined since he was a little kid wasn't going to happen. If he wanted to go to VT, he would have to walk on just like any other player off the street. He would then have to wait for an entire year to get a chance to play. Maybe. And then, *maybe* get a scholarship offer.

What did he have to do to make people believe in him?

He had been named an all-conference and an all-state player his junior year. He made over 40 percent of his threes. He knew he could play in college if somebody just gave him a chance.

As they continued to walk, Dell looked over at Steph and said, "Well, what's on your mind?"

"I don't want to sit out a year. I want to play." Steph said without hesitation.

Dell took a deep breath. "Can't say I blame you. You know that your mama and I love Virginia Tech. But..." Dell's voice trailed off into thought.

Steph looked up at his father. "But?"

Dell took another deep breath before he answered. "Let's just say I'm not so thrilled with my old school at this moment. Sometimes coaches have vision problems. They can't see what's right in front of them."

"So what do you think I should do?" Steph asked.

Dell stopped and looked directly at Steph. "That is up to you. But I think you already know the answer to your own question."

Steph thought about that as he and Dell got into the car to begin the long ride home from Blacksburg, Virginia.

He still had other options, but it was hard to let go of a lifelong dream. He had always imagined he would play for the Hokies, wearing number 30 in honor of his Pops. But, now?

He had a lot to think about.

Coach McKillop was drinking coffee in the Currys living room, making his case for why Steph should come and play at Davidson College. He had come to visit the Currys on a cool November day and he still couldn't believe his good luck. No major college basketball program had snatched Steph up.

Yet.

He still had a shot at a three-star recruit who was a five-star steal. He was sure of it.

McKillop looked at Steph, Dell, and Sonya, who were sitting on the living room sofa.

"Look, Steph," he said. "I believe that you can make an impact for us right away if you are willing to work hard."

"Davidson is small," he continued. "But on the upside, the academics are great. And every player that has played under me has graduated with a degree. Every. Last. One."

"I've already made my decision," Steph said evenly.

"Wait! I haven't even told you about how Davidson does all of its students' laundry for free!" Coach McKillop blurted out.

Everybody couldn't help but laugh, which broke some of the tension.

But the laughter died down quickly and soon Dell, Sonya, and Coach McKillop were staring directly at Steph, waiting for him to speak up. His parents weren't even sure what his final decision was. Of course he had talked to them about it, but he knew it was up to him.

Steph was a senior and his final basketball season with Charlotte Christian had just barely begun. And not one major college had knocked on his door.

Virginia Tech wasn't interested. None of the top schools thought he could play Division I ball. He was too small. He wasn't quick enough. Nobody had believed in him.

He had to make a decision.

It felt like the time when he was 14 years old and the youth pastor at church had told his youth group that each of them needed to make a decision. And they needed to do it on their own. He said that they needed to decide whether they were going to commit their life to God. That they needed to stand up and walk in front of the church and declare it before God and the church.

And it needed to be their decision alone. No parents. It was between them and God.

Steph knew that he had made the right decision when he walked up in front of the church to declare his commitment then and he knew he was making the right decision now.

"Well?" Dell, Sonya, and Coach McKillop said together.

Steph took a deep breath and smiled. "Where do I sign, Coach?"

Coach McKillop leapt out of his chair with a huge grin on his face. "Really?" he cried.

"Really," Steph replied.

Sonya ran over and hugged Steph as Dell laughed.

She turned to Coach McKillop and said, "We'll work on fattening him up for you. Promise."

Coach McKillop hugged Sonya then backed away a bit. He put his hand in hers, looked into her eyes and replied, "Don't worry, Sonya. I'll take him just the way he is. Really, he's fine just the way he is."

And that's when the tears started.

Unfinished Business

Steph felt like he had something to prove.

Of course, friends and family had been thrilled that he was going to Davidson, but he also got the impression that they felt like he had settled because the top-tier colleges had ignored him. There was a small part of him that couldn't help feeling that way, too. Sure, Davidson was a Division 1 school, but it was small, only about 1,600 students, and its heyday as a basketball power had been in the 1960s.

Steph thought about this as he and the Charlotte Christian Knights faced off against the Norcross High School Blue Devils at the 2005 Chick-Fil-A Classic Tournament in Columbia, South Carolina. It was a holiday tournament that featured some of the top high school teams in the nation.

It wasn't lost on Steph that they were on the court facing the #1 ranked high school in Georgia with a starting line-up filled with five-star recruits. He would be going toe-to-toe with Jodie Meeks, a highly regarded guard prospect who had signed on with basketball powerhouse, University of Kentucky.

It was two days before Christmas, but nobody expected a miracle for Charlotte Christian today. Norcross had already knocked off highly rated St. Anthony of New Jersey in a tense semifinal game that had gone to overtime. Most of those in attendance figured *that* game had been the real final and that Norcross would walk all over Charlotte Christian.

Steph started out slowly, but then caught fire. It seemed that he was all over the court and he couldn't miss. When he wasn't penetrating to make layups, he was making pinpoint passes to open players and then he was pulling up behind the three-point line and hitting momentum-deflating threes.

As the game wore on, people weren't talking about Jodie Meeks anymore. They were buzzing about the skinny kid who looked like he was

14 years old from the small Christian school. He was going to play for Davidson? *Davidson?* Really? Had none of the top college teams seen him play?

The game went back and forth, but when the final buzzer sounded, somehow, the Christmas miracle had happened. The score was Charlotte Christian 64, Norcross 60.

As his teammates jumped up and down and hugged on the court after the victory, Steph couldn't help but feel a bit vindicated. He had gone up against some of the best high school players in the nation and had proved that he not only belonged on the court with them, but that he could best them. Skinny, undersized, too small to play Steph Curry.

Size of your heart, he thought as he celebrated with his team.

Later, as he accepted the trophy for the most valuable player of the tournament, he tried to smile without looking too embarrassed. It felt a little awkward to accept the trophy because it had been a team effort that had led to this honor. It was never about one person. He wished he could give a little piece of the trophy to each of his teammates.

But he smiled as best he could as the pictures were taken, the congratulations were handed out, and hands were shaken.

And while all of this was going on he wasn't thinking about his last basketball season at Charlotte Christian or what the future might hold for him in college. He was thinking, *I'm hungry.* But this time it wasn't the hunger to prove he belonged. He was hungry for chicken nuggets and he couldn't wait for the hoopla to stop so he could *finally* go get some.

He had said it a thousand times before, but Steph was feeling it today. Today was the day that he was going to beat his Pops at H-O-R-S-E.

The car was packed up and Steph and his parents were getting ready to drop him off at Davidson to begin his next great adventure. But there was always time for a game of H-O-R-S-E before they took off. He had already beaten his Pops in one-on-one games. Steph had pointed out after he beat Dell the first time in a one-on-one, his Pops was old and slow and it wasn't fair to take advantage of the elderly.

Steph had smiled when he said it and so had Dell, but not so much.

But he still had never beaten his Dad at H-O-R-S-E.

Dell may have slowed over time, but he still hadn't lost his eagle-eye shot or his competitive edge. Steph remembered when his Pops hid behind the car and made an impossibly long shot that Steph could only shake his head at and say, "Really?"

Steph was dribbling the basketball on the family court with a familiar smile on his face when his dad came out of the house. Dell didn't even have to ask what was on Steph's mind. He walked onto the court shaking his head.

"You sure you want to start your first day of college like this, son? Crying in the car in the bitter arms of defeat?" Dell said laughing.

"Yes," Steph laughed in return. "It's called the perfect plan. You ever heard of it?" he replied quoting from one of his favorite movies, *Master of Disguise.* Steph had embraced his inner nerd long ago. "I'll even give you first shot."

Dell just shook his head again, "Okay. But don't say I didn't warn you."

Dell dribbled back about five feet behind the three line and let fly a shot that hit the front of the rim and bounced off.

Steph shook his head and smiled. "Thought you were going to make this hard for me."

He grabbed the ball, dribbled to the same spot, and let loose a high-arching jumper that hit nothing but net. Swish!

Dell grabbed the ball and dribbled to the same spot and let loose another shot. With the same result. He missed the shot! And even though Dell smiled, Steph could tell his dad was not happy with that shot at all.

From there it was on.

There were complicated and impossible fade-away shots. Reverse layups with three hand switches. Balls bounced off the court grabbed in midair and then banked into the basket. Crazy, no look hook shots, long distant bombs, balls bounced off the backboard and put back in with the left hand, shots from behind the basket. Each description of each shot was beginning to sound more and more like the rants of a crazy person as

Dell and Stephen went back and forth until the game was tied at H-O-R-S.

They were both laughing and trash talking, but they knew that beneath the surface, they both wanted to win—badly. It was a game within a game that they had been playing forever. Steph had learned long ago that while he and his Pops loved each other and would go to the ends of the earth for each other, when it came to playing H-O-R-S-E, they were competitors and true competitors played to win. His father had taught him that lesson since he could barely hold a basketball.

Dell missed his last shot and it was Steph's turn to call the shot.

He went back to the end of the court and made a run for the basket. He dribbled behind his back, dribbled between his legs, stopped three feet behind the three-point line, stepped back and fired a fade-away bomb that seemed to stop in mid-air before it sailed down and through the hoop without touching the rim.

Steph pointed to his Dad and said, "You have to do the ball work and the fade away."

Dell just smiled, nodded, and grabbed the ball. "I thought you were going to make this hard for me," he said, throwing Steph's earlier words back at him.

He walked back to the end of the court and made a slower run to the basket, dribbling behind his back, between his legs, stopping three feet behind the three-point line, mimicking Steph's moves exactly. He stepped back and shot the long fade away.

Steph watched as the ball seemed to fly in slow motion toward the basket. He could feel his teeth grinding as the ball hit the front of the rim, bounced softly to the backboard and then bounced back and hit the front of the rim again — and dropped harmlessly to the ground without going in.

Steph looked at the ball. Then he looked at Dell. And then he looked at the ball again in disbelief. He dropped to his knees and threw up his arms and shouted at the top of his lungs.

For the first time in his life, it was Steph: H-O-R-S, Dell: H-O-R-S-E!

Steph savored the victory for a moment and then

stood up and walked over to his father and gave him a hug. Dell smiled and said, "Well, I knew this day would come. Doesn't mean I have to like it. You deserved it. But, remember…"

Steph cut him off, "You are only as good as your last win."

Dell laughed as the two, arms over each other's shoulders, walked to the car to head to Davidson.

"By the way," Dell said to Steph, who was still grinning from ear to ear. "Your mom and I will meet you at Davidson. We'll be driving. You'll be walking. Not that I'm a sore loser or anything."

Steph was still smiling as he looked over at his Pops and saw that he wasn't smiling. He stopped smiling and then stopped in mid step. Dell looked directly at him and then started laughing as he said, "Get in the car."

Steph laughed again; he was already looking forward to the next H-O-R-S-E challenge that was sure to come.

Grounded Again

STEPH HAD ENDED HIS SENIOR YEAR basketball season at Charlotte Christian with impressive stats. He had been made all conference and all state again. His team had been runner-up for the state championship. He had ended up with a 48 percent shooting average from beyond the three line and he left Charlotte Christian with the Knight's all-time scoring record.

But now he was a freshman again and he was freaking out. He was running late for his first practice at Davidson's Belk Arena, where they played its regular season games.

He needed to get there quickly. He ran through the unfamiliar campus to the arena and somehow found the locker room. He hurriedly put on his practice gear and ran out without even bothering to tie his shoes. After taking a couple of wrong turns, he found the practice, which had already begun without him.

He knelt down and quickly tied his shoes, then stood up and stepped on to the court, breathing heavily.

"What are you doing, Mr. Curry?" Coach McKillop barked from the middle of the court.

Steph hung his head a little, then looked up and said, "Got a little turned around. I know I'm a few minutes late. I really apologize, Coach."

Coach McKillop eyes narrowed a bit as he said, "If you are going to play for Davidson, if you are going to play for *me,* you need to be on time. No excuses."

Stephen hung his head again. "Yes, sir. It won't happen again."

"No, it won't, Mr. Curry," McKillop said.

Steph nodded and took a couple of steps to where the other players were gathered.

"Whoa!" McKillop exclaimed. "And just where do you think you're going?"

Steph looked confused as he answered, "I'm going to practice, Coach."

McKillop shook his head. "No sir. If you're late you don't practice. Arriving late is disrespectful to me and is disrespectful to your teammates who arrived *on time.* I suggest you leave now and think very seriously about arriving at practice on time. *Tomorrow.*"

Steph froze on the court. He was completely mortified. Had he actually just been kicked out of the very first practice of his college career? It reminded him of when his mother hadn't let him play in his first middle school basketball game because he hadn't done the dishes the night before. This was the dishes, McKillop style. And Steph got the message, loud and clear; like his mother, Coach McKillop obviously ran a tight ship and you didn't mess with him.

Steph locked eyes with Coach McKillop, then his shoulders slumped slightly. "Yes, sir."

As he turned around and made his way to the gym exit he pledged that he would be at practice an hour early tomorrow and would never be late for practice again.

If he had bothered to turn around, he would have seen Coach McKillop's scowl slowly turn into an ever so slight grin as Steph

opened the gym door and disappeared into
the hallway.

Coach McKillop stood before a group of Davidson
alumni boosters and issued a glowing report about
their new freshman recruit. "Wait 'til you see
Stephen Curry," he told the group of boosters.
"He is going to be something special."

After his first unfortunate non-practice, Steph
had been true to his word and hadn't been late
again. Coach McKillop worked him hard, but he
always seemed to meet the challenge. During one
particularly grueling practice, McKillop waved
a white towel like a white flag in front of an
exhausted Steph's face and asked him, "Do
you surrender?"

Steph shook his head back and forth. He refused
to surrender. Coach McKillop believed the word
wasn't in his vocabulary.

But then came the first game of the 2006–07
season against Eastern Michigan. Steph was a
starter who was wearing jersey number 30 in honor
of his father. He wasn't doing so well

in his premier. He had 10 turnovers—*in the first half.*

McKillop could only wonder what the boosters were thinking now.

"Do you think we should take him out?" Assistant Coach Jim Fox asked Coach McKillop just before the halftime buzzer sounded. They were trailing Eastern Michigan by 18 points.

"No," McKillop answered decisively. McKillop was sure about this. He remembered the kid who had stunk up a court in a Las Vegas tournament, but who still had managed to keep his composure and his head up.

"He'll be fine," McKillop stated.

Steph came out the second half and settled down, eventually scoring 15 points and putting Davidson ahead for the first time after drilling a three-pointer with 2:35 remaining in the game. Davidson came back to win 81–77.

As the team was leaving the court to go to the locker room, Coach McKillop walked over to Steph, put his hands on his shoulders and said bluntly, "Thirteen turnovers in a game? Promise you aren't going to make that a habit." He hesitated, then pointed at his watch and said, "Remember the 12 o'clock rule."

Steph smiled slightly, looking down at the floor. "Right, Coach. I can only think about this game until midnight. Then I have to let it go. I promise, I'll do better next game."

McKillop just rubbed Steph's head and nodded, because he knew it was true. Steph kept his promises and he was just going to get better and better.

He looked down and saw that Steph had something scribbled in marker on the side of his shoe. The inscription read, "I can do all things..."

Coach McKillop smiled because he knew Steph and he knew the reference. It wasn't Steph bragging about himself, it was a Bible verse: Philippians 4:13. *I can do all things through Him that strengthens me.* Steph had told Coach McKillop that was his favorite Bible verse. Steph was putting his faith out there for all to see on the court. And while McKillop placed his faith in God, he also had faith in Steph Curry. He believed that Steph and the Davidson Wildcats were destined for great things.

That faith was justified after Steph scored 32 points against Michigan the very next game.

By the end of his freshman year, Steph led Davidson and the Southern Conference in scoring. Davidson won the Southern Conference and went to the 2007 NCAA tournament where they were knocked out in the first round against Maryland. He ended up the second-leading freshman scorer in the nation averaging 21.5 points per game behind Kevin Durant. He led all freshmen in three-pointers scored.

And at the end of Davidson's 2006–2007 season, people starting calling him the nickname that point guard Jason Richards had coined: the Baby-Faced Assassin.

Hard Decisions

STEPH LOOKED AT HIS HEAVILY TAPED WRIST and shook his head. It was killing him.

It was only a couple of days before Davidson was set to face #1 ranked University of North Carolina at the Time Warner Cable Arena in Charlotte. As the team warmed up before practice at Belk Arena, Coach McKillop, Dell Curry, and the team trainer, along with senior teammates Jason Richards and Tom Sanders, were huddled with Steph at the baseline, discussing whether he should play against UNC—or worse yet, whether he should sit out the 2007–2008 season entirely.

He had torn the cartilage in his left wrist and surgery had been given as an option to repair it. If he went ahead with the operation, the 2007–2008 season would be over for him. He was only a sophomore.

"Look, Steph," Coach McKillop said. "We'll miss

you if you opt for the surgery, that's no lie. But you have to think about yourself, too. You don't want to make this worse and wreck your future basketball career."

Dell nodded. He knew that Steph could have an NBA career ahead of him now. He hadn't been completely convinced of that until Steph's freshman year at Davidson. Now Steph was doing things in college that had taken Dell five years in the NBA to learn. Steph had also played for the silver medal— winning U-19 Team USA basketball team in the off-season—and had proven he could hold his own against international competition. He had even kept growing and at 6'3" he had come back to his sophomore season at Davidson a stronger and better player than the previous year.

Everything was seemingly going his way. But now this.

"It's up to you, son," Dell said. "I know it hurts and who knows if it will get better on its own? Just know that we all will support your decision, whatever it is."

Steph nodded, still looking at his heavily taped

wrist. He saw the concerned looks on Jason's and Tom's faces. He felt especially bad for Jason, who was point guard and his backcourt wing man. They were family. If he sat out the year, who knew what kind of year Davidson would have? Jason was a senior. It was his last year.

"Dude, we know it hurts a lot," Jason said. "I can see it in your face every time I pass you the ball. There's no shame in sitting out to let yourself heal."

Yes, the wrist hurt. It hurt a lot. But that would be nothing compared to the pain he would feel if he let the two players standing in front of him and the rest of the team down. And the injury wasn't in his shooting hand. He could adjust.

Steph looked directly at Jason and Tom and then scanned the concerned faces of the others surrounding him. "I can't let you guys down. Let's just keep the wrist taped and see how it goes. I can play through it."

"You don't have to do this, Steph," Jason said.

"Yes, I do," Steph replied. "I've made up my mind."

Coach McKillop put his hand on Steph's shoulder

and said, "Okay, Steph. Okay. But if it starts hurting too much, you have to let us know."

Steph nodded and said a silent prayer. But even as he prayed, he knew one thing for certain: his hand would pretty much have to fall off before he sat out this season and let his team down.
No matter how his sophomore season played out, he'd be there.

Steph's injured wrist did get better. By mid-season, he didn't need to tape it up. By the end of the regular season, he had led Davidson to the Southern Conference title and had been named Southern Conference Player of the Year. Steph and point guard Jason Richards became unstoppable in the backcourt. It was no coincidence that Steph led the nation in threes and Jason led the nation in assists.

Despite those stats, when Davidson was placed 10th seed in the Midwest Regional of the NCAA college basketball playoffs, most people assumed that they would probably be one-and-done just like the previous year when they lost to Maryland in the first round.

But it is called March Madness for a reason.

There were only 16.8 seconds left to play in the Midwest Regional championship game. The winner of this Elite 8 game would go on to play in a Final Four game and have a shot at taking it all: an NCAA championship.

The entire country was holding its breath: Would it be Kansas or would it be Davidson?

Davidson was the Cinderella story of the 2008 NCAA Basketball Tournament. Millions of college basketball fans who had dismissed Davidson at the beginning of the tournament were now asking seriously, "Can they do it? Can Davidson beat Kansas and go to the Final Four?"

Steph Curry had been responsible for Davidson's seemingly impossible run of defeating Gonzaga, Georgetown, and Wisconsin on its way to this Elite 8 game against Kansas. And suddenly, fans and sportscasters were asking how all of the major colleges in the country had let Steph Curry slip through their fingers. In the span of two weeks, he had become the most talked about college basketball player in the nation.

Steph had racked up 40 points against Gonzaga, 30 points against Georgetown, and 33 points against Wisconsin. Shots from downtown. Impossible twisting layups. Soft touch mid-shots. Steph was on fire and was burning down elite basketball programs in his path.

Everybody was buzzing about Davidson's Baby Faced Assassin. The whole world now knew what Steph had known since middle school: *just give him the ball and they will win this game.*

Nobody had given Davidson a chance in the NCAA Tournament. The Wildcats had played a tough non-conference schedule against basketball powerhouses like University of North Carolina, Duke, and UCLA earlier in the season. And they had lost to all of them. But after years of losing one-on-one games against his father's teammates, Steph knew that you can learn more from losing than you can from winning.

And Steph believed. It was as if the Bible verse he had inscribed on his shoes had leapt off of his feet and had come to life. He could, indeed, do all things.

In the first game against #7 seed Gonzaga, he scored 30 of his 40 points in the second half and sank a critical three-pointer to put Davidson ahead 77–74 with less than a minute left in the game. He saw his parents in the stands cheering wildly and pointed to them after the basket. *Thanks for believing in me.*

Davidson 82 – Gonzaga 76

Steph still believed when his team was down 11 points at the end of the first half against #2 seed Georgetown. Once again, he started slow, but scored 25 of his 30 points in the second half.

Davidson 74 – Georgetown 70

Steph believed while Davidson unexpectedly buried #3 seed Wisconsin at Detroit's Ford Field. He made a believer of LeBron James, who was sitting in the stands watching the unlikely miracle unfold.

Davidson 73 – Wisconsin 56

And now just 16.8 seconds were left and Davidson had the ball in the Midwest Regional Final against #1 seed Kansas. They were down 59–57. It was Davidson against Goliath once again, and Davidson would have the last shot to either tie or win the game. The stands were filled with red Davidson shirts and people holding signs saying: We Believe!

When Coach McKillop called Davidson's last timeout, Kansas and everybody at Ford Field—everybody in the entire nation—knew exactly who the ball was going to for that final shot.

Steph knew it was up to him. He had scored 25 hard-earned and exhausting points against a Kansas defense that used four different guards to defend him. He was out of gas. It reminded him of the time Coach McKillop waved a towel in front of him during an exhausting freshman practice and asked him if he was ready to surrender.

No way. Not then. Not now. Not ever.

As Coach McKillop drew out the play for a high screen at the top of the key to get him a look for that last shot, Steph rested his hand on Bryant Barr's shoulder. Bryant was his roommate and his best friend. They attended church together on Sunday. It was good to know that his friend in faith and life would be out there with him. Forward

Steve Rossiter, another good friend and compatriot in many of Steph's college pranks, was by his side. Jason Richards and Steph exchanged glances briefly. They both knew how big this moment was.

When the buzzer sounded to resume play, Steph felt calm. Win or lose he wasn't alone. His family was with him on the court.

Steph inbounded the ball to Steve Rossiter in the backcourt and Steve immediately passed the ball back to Steph. He dribbled the ball up the court. He was shadowed by Kansas guard Brandon Rush. As Steph passed midcourt, he darted to the left, trying to pick up the screen that teammate Thomas Sander had set. As Steph cut, Rush fell down, but he was picked up by Kansas guard Mario Chalmers.

Steph didn't have a look. Only six seconds left in the game!

He cut back to the right, but Chalmers easily got past a second screen that Thomas tried to set. As Steph moved to try to get free, Rush got back up and now Steph was being hounded by both Chalmers and Rush.

Steph moved to the right side of the court past

the three-point line and stopped. Time seemed to stop. Rush and now Kansas guard Sherron Collins ran toward him. He still didn't have a good look. Only three seconds left! Should he take the shot anyway? He had made so many improbable shots in the tournament. Could he pull out one more? Should he take the shot or not?

Steph saw Jason Richards at the top of the key, 25 feet from the basket, unguarded. Everybody expected Steph to take the last shot, but Jason had the best look.

He knew what he had to do in that moment. He pump-faked a shot and then passed the ball off to Jason. *Trust, Commitment, Care.* Steph trusted Jason with the game on the line. With only 1.3 seconds left on the clock Jason took the shot from behind the three line.

It seemed like the ball was up in the air for an eternity as Steph watched it arc up and then head down toward the basket. The crowd had grown silent as fans from both sides held their breath and waited. Would the miracle happen? Steph looked down as Jason fell onto his back after releasing the shot. Jason was putting his hands over his face. It was then that he knew what Jason knew.

The shot was off.

Steph looked back at the rim as the ball bounced off the backboard to the left and the game-ending buzzer sounded.

Davidson had missed the miracle by six inches. Kansas had ended Davidson's impossible run.

Jason stayed on the ground with his hands over his face while Kansas celebrated. Bryant Barr ran over to pick him up, then Steve Rossiter and Thomas Sander followed. There were tears in Jason's eyes. Steph looked out at the sea of red Davidson shirts in the crowd, the top of his jersey in his mouth.

But instead of downcast faces, he saw people applauding. The signs were still hoisted high: We Believe! Instead of silence there was cheering. Davidson students were yelling, "Great run!" and "Keep your heads up!"

Steph was disappointed that the run was over, but he wasn't completely devastated. He looked up in the seats and saw his entire family, his mom and dad and Seth and Sydel, applauding the Davidson team. And even though Davidson had lost today, Steph knew that there would be other days and other games.

As he walked off the court, the disappointment and sadness still weighing on him, he knew one thing: he was surrounded by family. Family was always there for you in good times and bad.

And regardless what the future held, Davidson was family—now and forever.

Good Times

Bryant Barr was sitting in the Commons, Davidson's favorite social hub, waiting for Steph to show up.

He had seen some news on the internet that had surprised him and he needed to talk to Steph about it. When he first read it, he could hardly believe that Steph hadn't said a word about it. They were roommates. They were best friends. How could he not have mentioned anything to him?

Of course, maybe Steph had lost track in the media frenzy that followed Davidson's amazing run into the Elite 8 and near upset of Kansas. Steph had been swamped with requests to come to late-night talk shows and people everywhere were asking him for autographs. It seemed like there was a never-ending stream of reporters who wanted to come on campus to interview him.

Steph seemed genuinely surprised by all of the

attention. Bryant shook his head. Only Steph would have a year like he had and wonder what the big deal was all about. He was handling it well. He always treated autograph seekers with respect. After all, he had grown up with a father who had been a public figure for years, so it wasn't unfamiliar to him.

He smiled as he watched Steph walking up to him with his usual turkey sandwich, wearing earbuds.

Steph took one of his earbuds out and looked perplexed. "What?" he asked Bryant.

"You think you'd have eaten all the turkey in North Carolina by now. Do you ever order anything else for lunch?" Bryant replied.

Steph laughed. "Nope."

He sat down next to Bryant and said, "So, what's up?"

Bryant cleared his throat. "Well, I read something on the internet about you that took me by surprise. I thought maybe you might enlighten me about it."

Steph look surprised and confused, then blurted

out, "Look, I'm coming back to Davidson next year, okay? They say all kinds of crazy things."

There was talk that Steph might go pro and not come back for his junior year, but that was not what Bryant wanted to talk about. "That's great news, Steph," Bryant replied.

"But you know that's not what I'm talking about. Don't play dumb."

The confused look on Stephen's face deepened. "I seriously do not know what you are talking about," he said.

Bryant rolled his eyes, then looked at Steph again. "You were voted as a finalist for the John Wooden Award for the best college player in the nation and you don't mention it to anybody? You didn't even tell me? Really?"

Steph had an embarrassed look on his face. "Oh, that," he replied. "Guess it never came up in conversation. I'm only a finalist. I may not win it. Didn't want to make a big deal out of it."

"Reaalllly?" Bryant said, stretching out the word. He started laughing. "You're a bonehead. You know that, don't you?"

Steph started laughing along with him. "Yep. I have you as a friend."

The two were laughing so hard that other students looked over at them, trying to figure out what was so funny. When the laughter finally died down Bryant put his hand on Steph's shoulder.

"There's something else," Bryant said, suddenly serious. "I'm getting involved in something called Nothing But Nets. It's a United Nations program that purchases pesticide-covered mosquito nets to help stop the spread of malaria in Africa. Every two minutes, a child dies of malaria in Africa. Every. Single. Day."

Steph remembered the stories Bryant had told him about a mission trip he had taken to Africa. The stories had been touching and tragic.

"I've got this idea for a three-on-three tournament to raise funds to help buy some nets for them," Bryant continued. "I was wondering if you'd like to help out."

Steph looked Bryant in the eye and flashed a smile. "You know the answer. What can I do to help?"

* * * * *

Steph was a little nervous. He was sending Ayesha a Facebook message to see if she wanted to get together again with him since he was in Los Angeles to attend the 2008 ESPN ESPY Awards being held at the Kodak Theater. It had been a whirlwind after the NCAA Tournament and he had been nominated for Breakout Athlete of the Year.

It had been a long time since Ayesha had handed Steph those Maynard's Fuzzy Peaches at youth group, but he hadn't forgotten it. Ayesha wasn't allowed to date in high school, so they never really got together. He had the impression she didn't think much of athletes anyway.

They had kind of lost contact since he had gone on to Davidson and she had moved to Los Angeles after graduation to pursue an acting career.

He had actually contacted her two weeks earlier on Facebook when he was in town for a basketball camp. He had sent a message asking if they could get together and see each other.

Her reply had been disappointing. She said that

she was sorry, but she couldn't get together with him. Maybe next time.

Maybe next time. Steph smiled a little as he waited for a reply from Ayesha this time. He was pretty sure she wasn't expecting *next time* to be two weeks later.

The reply came faster than he expected:

You're back in Los Angeles? That was fast. Why?

Steph typed back:

ESPY Award Ceremony. I'm up for an award.

Ayesha replied:

Why are you up for one?

Steph smiled. It was kind of refreshing. It was obvious that Ayesha had no idea what had happened during the NCAA Tournament. She probably hadn't even watched any of the games.

Steph typed:

I'll explain when we get together. C'mon. It'll be fun. Catch up on old times.

There was a long pause that made Steph uncomfortable. Then the new reply popped up:

Okay. We can get a chai latte or something. I'll show you around.

Steph balled up his fist and made a "Yes!" gesture.

He typed:

Great! Let me know where to pick you up. Looking forward.

After they exchanged information, Steph closed his laptop and leaned back in his hotel room chair. It would be fun to hang with Ayesha again.

Steph sat at the black round table with his mother and father at the 2009 NBA draft at Madison Square Garden in New York. He smiled briefly at Ayesha, who was also at the table with his family.

She was his girlfriend now. Things had worked out pretty well since that first "date" in Los Angeles a year ago.

He was nervous.

He felt that he was ready to play in the NBA. That's why he had decided to leave Davidson and put his name in for the NBA draft after his junior season. It had been a tough decision, and he felt it was the right one. When he had sat down with his teammate and friend Steve Rossiter at the

Commons in 2009 and told him he wasn't coming back for his senior year, it had been hard. It was even harder to tell Coach McKillop, who had molded him into the player he had become.

It hadn't been entirely unexpected. Coach McKillop had been happy for him, but said, "You are coming back to get your degree, right? I'm not going to have you wreck my perfect graduation record."

Steph laughed and promised that he would as the two hugged.

But after he announced his intentions, it all started again: the doubters started coming out of the woodwork.

Experts doubted whether he had what it took to play in the NBA. Even though he had grown to 6'3," he was still too small to be an effective point guard. He was too thin and would get battered in the pros. He wasn't good enough on defense. Sure, he was good with long threes when he was wide open, but could he make those shots when tenacious NBA-caliber defenders were in his face?

Maybe they doubted because Davidson hadn't made it to the 2009 NCAA Tournament at all. Maybe the miracle run in the tournament the year before had been a fluke. Still, Steph had been the leading scorer in the nation in his junior year. That had to count for something, right?

Rumor had it that he was going to get drafted by the Golden State Warriors. His agent wouldn't even let him work out with the Warriors before the draft. And he knew that their current point guard, Monte Ellis, had made it clear that he was not happy about Steph coming on the team. The Warriors were a train wreck.

Steph really wanted to get drafted by the New York Knicks. His dad and his agent wanted him to go to the New York Knicks.

But it wasn't going to happen. The Warriors had the 7th pick.

In their hotel before the draft, Steph was expressing doubts about going to the Warriors, but as usual, his mother put it in perspective. "It's a blessing just to get drafted. You have been looking forward to this day for your whole life, so you go where you are drafted and you do the best job you can. God has his reasons."

Steph had no doubt about that. He just prayed that God could maybe pull off a little miracle for him and get him on the Knicks.

When NBA Commissioner David Stern made the announcement that the Golden State Warriors had taken Steph in the 7th round, it took nobody by surprise. Instead of going to New York City, he was going all the way across the country to Oakland, California.

Steph smiled, stood up, straightened his grey three-piece suit and hugged Ayesha. He was given a Warriors cap and he dutifully put it on as he walked up to the podium to shake hands with Stern to officially become a member of the Warriors.

It wasn't his first choice but he was grateful. And he was going to make the best out of it.

A Test of Faith

RIGHT BEFORE THE WARRIORS' OPENING NIGHT GAME against the Suns, Steph was sitting with Bob Myers and Coach Jackson and was about so sign his contract. He was excited but kept his cool, thinking, *man, I'll be able to take care of my family with this.* A few years later, people would criticize the deal he was making. But before his first game, in that hotel room, Steph felt blessed knowing that he'd be playing in the NBA for at least four years, and he thought to himself, *let's see where it goes from there.*

When he lifted the pen he remembered what his dad told him: "You never count another man's money. It's what you've got and how you take care of it."

Steph smiled. He said to himself, *if I'm complaining about $44 million over four years, then I've got other issues in my life.*

He signed the contract.

Things had been going good for Steph in the NBA
until his ankles betrayed him. The Warriors had
been terrible his first season, but he had led the
NBA in three pointers, been named to the NBA
Rookie All-Star Team, and he had been runner-up
for the Rookie of the Year award.

It had been a good season overall, but that had
been 2009–2010.

It was now 2012 and Steph was sitting in his
living room looking at the cast on his right ankle,
wondering if he would ever be able to play in the
NBA again. It worried him. It had been the second
surgery on his ankle in two seasons. Last season, he
managed to keep playing despite spraining his ankle
seven times. He'd still managed to average
19 points and six assists a game.

He had surgery on the ankle at the end of the
season to repair and strengthen the tendons. Then
he worked hard in the off-season to rehab the ankle
to get him ready for the next season. He'd been
everywhere and seen practically everybody who

might have a clue as to how to help him recover completely.

The ankle had been feeling pretty good as the new season began, but then disaster struck again. He rolled the same ankle in an exhibition game against the Sacramento Kings. Then he sprained it again in the second game of the season against the Chicago Bulls. He kept reinjuring the ankle and had to sit out more games. By March his season was over and he needed another surgery.

He had only played in 26 games the entire 2011–2012 season.

Reporters were already talking about how the promising career of Steph Curry was over. Only three years in the NBA and people were saying he was washed up.

He knew he should put his faith in God, but he couldn't help but be frightened. What if his NBA career was over? He looked over at Ayesha who was sitting on the couch reading. They had just gotten married last year and they were expecting their first baby in July.

What would the future hold? What would it mean for his new and growing family if his career was over? It was overwhelming sometimes.

Steph thought about what his mother might tell him. She always said that God has a plan for everybody. Just put yourself in God's hands. She was his rock during hard times. She had always emphasized that God and family come first and that sports should never be your top priority in life.

She would also probably tell him to stop feeling sorry for himself and get out and do the work to make things better. She had always been a firm believer that God helps those who help themselves.

Steph knew what he had to do. He looked at his cell phone resting on the table beside him. He picked it up and hit speed dial.

After a few rings, Sonya picked up on the other end.

Steph hesitated then said, "Hey, Mom. Do you have a few minutes? I need to talk."

There was a momentary silence, then Sonya replied. "You know I'm always here for you, baby. What do you need?"

Steph cleared his throat and the words rushed out.

MVP

THREE YEARS PASSED. Steph looked out at the audience. He felt like he was living in a dream. Three years ago, he wasn't even sure if he was going to have an NBA career because of his injuries. Today, he was standing before an audience ready to give his acceptance speech for the 2014–2015 NBA Most Valuable Player Award.

He cleared his throat as he gazed out. The audience was filled with people he loved. There was his mother and father and Seth and Sydel. Even his Grandmother Candy had showed up. Grandma Duckie couldn't make it, but he was sure she was watching on television from The Grottoes. She would probably be switching back and forth between his speech and the Atlanta Braves baseball game if he knew her.

He thought about the old rim nailed to the utility pole his Pops had learned to shoot on. He wondered if Grandaddy Jack was looking down at him. He felt like he was.

So many people to thank. He didn't even know where to start.

He looked at Ayesha and smiled at her. Who knew that day they spent together in Los Angeles would lead to love and marriage and family? Their daughter Riley was sitting on her lap. She was almost three and had his mother's eyes. Riley was a handful. Not shy, that one. And another baby was on the way. He was blessed.

There was his Pops who taught him how to play the game right. Next to him was his mom who taught him that there are many paths and who would have supported him no matter what he had chosen to do with his life. She was tough, too. He had learned his grit from her. She still fined him $100 for every turnover he made in games.

He glanced at Seth. He had played so many one-on-one games with Seth until they were called inside because the neighbors had complained about the noise or Seth had stomped off accusing him of cheating by not giving him a foul. He smiled at Sydel. How many ridiculous movies had he watched with her, until he knew the lines by heart?

He loved them all.

Those who weren't in the audience were in his heart.

He was thankful for Coach Shonn Brown. Where it all began.

He could practically feel the tattoo on his wrist as Coach McKillop jumped into his thoughts. When he was at Davidson he had gotten the letters TCC tattooed on his wrist. The number 30 was right under the letters. The number was his father's jersey number—and now it was his.

TCC: Trust Commitment Care. He owed so much to Coach McKillop who not only pushed him to excellence on the court, but taught him the more valuable lessons of how to live his life.

So many to thank.

Bryant Barr, his best friend, who kept it real. They had actually met President Obama and talked to him about the Nothing But Nets program. Bryant's small idea had grown into something bigger than both of them. Steph donated a net for every point he scored from the three-point line. He had never been so proud to give.

Of course, there were his teammates on the Warriors. If he could, he would chop up the MVP trophy and split it 14 ways. In some ways, Steph felt that there was no such thing as an MVP; basketball was a team effort and they were all MVPs.

And this was a great group of guys. They had the best record in the NBA and were set to face the Memphis Grizzlies in the playoffs after getting by the New Orleans Pelicans.

He had a great coach in Steve Kerr and heck, even the greatest equipment manager in the world. They were all part of the equation that added up to this award. Everybody was an MVP. Everybody deserved this award.

It was humbling. It was time to thank all who had made this journey possible.

Steph took a deep breath, stepped up to the microphone and began to speak.

"First and foremost, I have to thank my Lord and Savior Jesus Christ for blessing me with the talents to play this game, with a family that supports me day in and day out. I'm his humble servant right now. I can't say it enough: how important my faith is to how I play the game and who I am, so—I'm just blessed and I'm thankful for where I am…"

The First
Championship Ring

IT WAS SURREAL.

Steph and the rest of the Golden State Warriors were standing behind President Obama in the White House. They were there to be recognized for their 2014–2015 NBA Championship season.

And Obama was talking trash about him.

"For those of you who watched the game against the Wizards last night, he was—to use slang— he was clowning," Obama said. He then did an imitation of Steph jumping up and down.

Steph had to laugh. There was a good reason to celebrate the victory over the Washington Wizards the night before. Steph had scored 51 points and the Warriors had won again, bringing their record to 45–4. This season, people were saying they were on track to break the 1995–1996 game-winning record of the Chicago Bulls of 72 games. Steph believed they could win 73 this year.

He couldn't help but be proud. The Warriors had come a long way. They had gone from awful to awesome in just a few years. He had worked hard to come back from his ankle injuries and had found a company that made an ankle brace that really helped him. It hadn't been easy, but it's rare that anything you really want comes easily. He had learned that his whole life.

The Warriors had believed he would come back. They signed him to a four-year contract extension the very next year, despite the missed playing time and the injuries.

He thought back to the Summer of Tears back in Charlotte and all of those hours in the gym working on changing his jump shot. He had worked through it. He hadn't given up. The hard work, sweat, and faith had paid off. He had broken the NBA single season record for three-pointers two seasons ago. Then he proceeded to break his own three-point record during the championship season.

There had been hard bumps in the road, but

his family had been there for him, supporting him through the good times and the bad.

It was a bit of a miracle, he thought. Three years ago people were saying that he might never play another NBA game. That he was done.

God certainly does work in mysterious ways, Steph marveled.

He'd always believed in his team. He knew that they would pull through even when they were down 2–1 to the Memphis Grizzlies in the playoffs. He knew that his team had the grit to beat the Houston Rockets in the Western Conference Finals, even though they were a smaller team. And when they were down 2–1 against the Cleveland Cavaliers in the NBA Finals. Steph had never given up. His team had never given up. They roared back to win the next three games to take the series in six games.

He looked back at Klay Thompson and laughed after President Obama said that he thought that maybe Klay's jump shot was prettier than Steph's. He and Klay had been dubbed "The Splash Brothers" by a sports writer and the name had stuck. After all, they both did drain a lot of baskets from the three line. Splash!

Steph understood Klay in a way that maybe nobody else could. Both of their fathers had been NBA players and both of their mothers had played volleyball in college. Neither of them had been all that highly touted when they played in high school. Although Klay always teased that *he* had been a four-star recruit and Steph had only been a three-star recruit.

President Obama teased him about the golf match he had lost to the President the previous year. At the time, Steph thought that was the coolest thing he'd ever done. Golf with the President of the United States!

But then he changed his mind after he brought back the Larry O'Brien NBA Championship Trophy to share with Davidson. He decided not to tell the media he was going, but of course everybody on campus found out and it was standing room only at the Davidson Performing Arts Center.

The crowd chanted "MVP! MVP!" as he showed up on the stage holding the trophy. It was a little embarrassing, but it felt so good to be back home again.

Even when Coach McKillop teased him about not finishing his degree yet.

"You're going to get it, right?" he said.

"Yes, Coach. Promise," Steph replied with a slight smile.

Now *that* was the coolest thing ever.

As Steph looked out at the audience that had gathered at the White House to honor the Warriors, he couldn't help but think that this was going to be a special year for them. They were working like a well-oiled machine and they had been unstoppable so far. A repeat of last year was not out of the question. They had a fantastic championship season last year and this season was looking even better.

Keep it humble, Steph thought after the President finished talking and the gathering broke up. *You never know what's going to happen.*

"Ready to go home?" Ayesha asked as she took his arm while stragglers milled around the room.

It had been a busy day. It had been an amazing day.

But, all in all, Steph couldn't wait to get home and be with his kids.

Family

WITH 10.6 SECONDS LEFT IN THE GAME, Steph knew he had to come up big. He had missed his last three-point attempt as Cleveland Cavaliers center Kevin Love came out and dogged him from above the three-point line. Steph was surprised that they had put the big man on him, but he had to admit that Love had done a great job staying on him.

Pretty agile for a guy who is 6'10."

It was game 7 of the NBA Championship and it was all on the line. The Warriors were behind 89–93 and even if Steph was able to knock down a three, they would still be one point down. If he could get Iman Shumpert, who was guarding him, to foul while he took his three, there was still a chance to tie up the game with a four-point play. At the very least, the Warriors needed a quick three so they would have a chance to get one last possession.

It was a slim chance, but it was a chance and Steph never discounted miracles.

Shumpert was on Steph for the inbound pass on the Warrior's side of the court. Iman was taller than Steph and it would be tough to get a shot off against him and his long reach.

Steph got loose and Andre Iguodala inbounded to him. Shumpert was all over him, but he dribbled forward, then made a quick side-step to lose him above the three-point line. Just enough separation to throw up the three.

He knew as soon as he threw it up the game was over. He had thrown up so many threes he could feel when the shot was off. The ball missed badly and ricocheted off to the right. Teammate Marreese Speights grabbed the rebound in the corner and tried to shoot another three, but it was too late. As the ball bounced harmlessly off the rim, the Cavaliers started celebrating.

LeBron James was on his hands and knees on the court weeping.

As Steph watched the celebration unfold on the court with the shocked home fans at Oracle

Stadium, he knew he hadn't had a great game. He had scored 17 points tonight, which was a good game for most players, but the Warriors had needed a great game from him and he hadn't delivered.

As he got in the car to go home he couldn't help but feel the sting of the loss. The Golden State Warriors had been ahead three games to one in the series. No team in the history of the NBA Finals had come back from a 3–1 deficit to win a championship.

Until Cleveland did. Today.

Sometimes you don't win. Sometimes you have bad games. That's sports. Last year the Warriors had beaten the Cavaliers to take the championship. This year it was Cleveland's turn. Still, it stung. He probably wouldn't watch the recording of game 7 for a while.

As he leaned in to get into the driver's seat of the car, he kissed his wife Ayesha on the cheek. He looked in the back seat and saw his two daughters, Riley and Ryan, strapped safely into their car seats.

He couldn't help but smile a little. Sure, the Warriors had lost, but he had been taught by his mother and father throughout his life that God and family come first. And, while he loved playing basketball, he loved his family even more.

He looked at three-year-old Riley, who had become something of a media star herself and rubbed her head.

His daughters were still young. They came to games, but they still didn't understand about wins and losses. It was all a big show to them. He remembered being really young and sitting in arenas watching his father, Dell, play for the Charlotte Hornets.

He was looking at a new generation of Currys growing up around the NBA.

He took a deep breath and said to his daughter, "We lost, Riley."

Riley looked directly at her father and said matter-of-factly, "I know, Daddy." She hesitated for a moment, then added, "But that's okay."

But that's okay. Steph smiled.

He remembered what his father, Dell Curry, a 16-year veteran NBA player, had taught him during the many games of H-O-R-S-E they had played against each other while he was growing up: you are only as good as your last victory. So you have to keep on improving. You have to keep on proving yourself.

Steph's mother, Sonya, had taught him that he should place his faith in God during good times and bad. There are always ups and downs. It's what you learn from the downs that show what kind of person you are.

No matter the ending it had been an exceptional year. He had accepted the NBA Most Valuable Player award for a second consecutive year. The Warriors had set the NBA season win record with a 73–9 record for the 2015–2016 season. Steph owned the NBA record for the most three-pointers in a single season, yet again.

But, even after this phenomenal season, they had lost the NBA Championship to LeBron James and Cleveland.

That was the way of it, sometimes.

He slipped into the driver's seat and started the car. His father, mother, sister, and brother would be at his house waiting for him. There wouldn't be the loud celebrations of last year, but he knew his family would be there to support him, nonetheless.

He looked back at Riley and said, "Time to go home."

The smile she beamed back at him was worth more than a thousand NBA Championship rings.

The Second Ring

S<small>TEPH WALKED INTO</small> C<small>HARLOTTE</small> C<small>HRISTIAN</small> H<small>IGH</small> S<small>CHOOL</small> auditorium, and the memories swept over him. The packed crowd was cheering when he stepped onto the stage.

He was one of them once. This was the place where his dreams had begun to take shape. He was thankful and wanted to share his life lessons with the excited young students.

He remembered what Coach Brown had told him one evening at his office: That he wasn't ready to play varsity. That he was too small and too skinny. And he remembered his disappointment and his determination to prove the coach wrong.

"In my freshman year," he told the students, "I went through some doubts about whether I could play on the varsity level. One of my only regrets is not trying out for varsity that year. I played JV. That taught me to go for it. To not let what people might

tell you—no matter how short or skinny
you might be—deter you from getting where you
want to go."

When he spoke, he thought about the Warriors'
last season. How he and the team had to rebound
from losing the championship.

On July 1, 2016, Steph and his teammates—
Clay Thompson, Draymond Green, Andre Iguodala,
Coach Steve Kerr, and GM Myers—came to the
Hamptons to meet Kevin Durant. In their mind,
Durant was the final piece of a team in a search of
another championship.

The meeting went great. Durant loved the way
the Warriors played. They had fun with the game
and played freely, and he was impressed by the way
their games touched so many people.

When Durant met the guys, he felt that their
energy was pure. It was a feeling he couldn't
ignore. He wanted to be a part of it.

Steph was the megastar that started the surge of
the team to the top, yet he was willing to share the
superstar spotlight, and he wrote a welcoming text
message that sealed the deal.

People had doubts about how well Durant would do with Steph and Clay and the rest of the team, but Steph knew it would work out just fine. Steph wanted to make the team better and he knew that to make it work he would have to do his part. His teammates took note of all of this. Outside the team, people didn't fully appreciate it, but the Warriors sure did. Especially Durant, who had to live with his own expectations and pressure. Steph, being himself, did his best to make it work, and they both thrived. For Steph, the team always came first, and Kevin Durant came to appreciate that.

Durant's integration was seamless because everyone on the team made it possible. But he appreciated Steph's cooperation the most. Durant was impressed that Steph was willing to sacrifice being the biggest star on the team and that he was selfless and caring about his teammates. "Caring about other people is real," Durant said. "It's not fake. It's not a façade. Steph doesn't put on this mask."

At the beginning of the season, there was a point where Steph tried to analyze and control the situation of playing with Durant, and make sure everybody on the team was happy and getting shots. He felt the responsibility to make the point that it's about the team, not about himself. But then came the Christmas Day game against the Cavaliers. The Warriors were leading but at the last three seconds Kyrie Irving's jumper ended the game, 109–108 for the Cavaliers. Kevin Durant led all players with 36 points and 15 rebounds, while Klay Thompson and Draymond Green contributed 24 and 16 points, respectively, and Steph added a modest 15 points.

Thinking about the game, Steph realized that the team had such high-IQ players that if he could be more aggressive and do what he needed to do every single night, then everything would flow naturally. He now had a clear vision of what he should do for the team. Once Steph made this decision, the road to the second championship was cleared.

On Monday June 12, 2017 at the Oracle Arena, the Golden State Warriors finished the job. The Warriors capped the greatest three-year run in regular season history with the greatest post season on record in NBA history: 16–1, a three-sweep stampede to the Finals and then a powerful 4–1 dismantling of LeBron James' Cavaliers. Steph's past three seasons were a blast: 207 regular season wins. Two championships. Two MVPs. A scoring title. Going 16–1 in the playoffs, beating LeBron James twice. Steph and the Warriors had not only redefined the way basketball was played, but also the way it was watched, and created the golden opportunity to dominate the game for years to come.

After the winning game, Steph was all smiles during the amazing moments in the middle of the arena with his kids, who were decked out in Warriors gear. He embraced his adorable daughters, Riley, four, and Ryan, nearly two. His father, his mother, his wife Ayesha, sister Sydel and brother Seth were all in attendance smiling, cheering, and enjoying the moment. Steph felt truly blessed. Nobody had believed he could reach so high when he was growing up. People had said he wasn't tall enough. He was too skinny. He wasn't tough enough to compete with the best. He couldn't play for top college teams. He was injury prone. He was too soft to be an impact player in the NBA. Steph had heard it all. And it made him work harder to prove the doubters wrong. He had spent his entire life proving that he belonged on the court.

And he was proving again that he was one of the best players on the planet. At age 29 he made his mark on the history of the sport, and he had done it his way. With great talent, courage through thick and thin, and faith in God, he showed every small and skinny kid who loves to play the game that they too can dream big, and one day become champions.

Also by Rick Leddy

LeBron James: The King of the Game

The U.S. Women's Soccer Team Road to Glory:
American Heroes

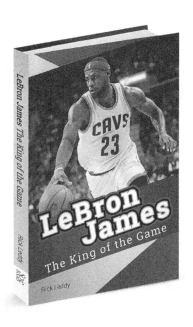

LeBron James – The King of the Game

By Rick Leddy

LeBron James is the shy son of a teenage mother, both wandering, constantly searching for a home and fighting to survive. When LeBron's immense talent is finally discovered, he seizes the opportunity and changes his life forever. This is the heartfelt story of a young boy's incredible rise to glory to become the world's best basketball player through the power of family, friendship, and love.

Rick Leddy is an author, cartoonist, poet, and blogger. His columns have appeared in the *Los Angeles Times* and *The Orange County Register*. His regular comic features appeared in *Box Office Magazine* and the *Los Angeles View*.

Ages 9 and up

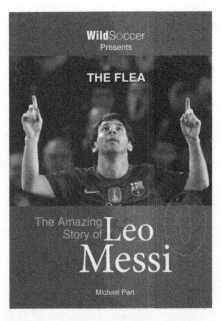

The Flea – The Amazing Story of Leo Messi

By Michael Part

The captivating story of soccer legend Lionel Messi, from his first touch at age five in the streets of Rosario, Argentina, to his first goal on the Camp Nou pitch in Barcelona, Spain. *The Flea* tells the amazing story of a boy who was born to play the beautiful game and destined to become the world's greatest soccer player. The best-selling book by Michael Part is a must read for every soccer fan!

Ages 9 and up

HAVE YOU READ THE FIRST BOOK?
GET IT NOW!

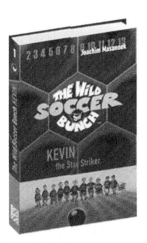

THE WILD SOCCER BUNCH
BOOK 1
KEVIN the Star Striker

When the last of the snow has finally melted, soccer season starts!

Kevin the Star Striker and the *Wild Soccer Bunch* rush to their field. They have found that Mickey the bulldozer and his gang, the *Unbeatables*, have taken over. Kevin and his friends challenge the *Unbeatables* to the biggest game of their lives.

Can the *Wild Soccer Bunch* defeat the *Unbeatables*, or will they lose their field of dreams forever? Can they do what no team has done before?

More from Sole Books

The best-selling Soccer Stars series
by Michael Part

The Flea: The Amazing Story of Leo Messi

Cristiano Ronaldo: The Rise of a Winner

Neymar the Wizard

James Rodriguez: The Incredible Number 10

Balotelli: The Untold Story

Luis Suarez: A Striker's Story

www.solebooks.com

Made in the USA
Las Vegas, NV
02 September 2023

76955899R00094